Mr Wumble
and
the Dragon
and
Other Stories

by
ENID BLYTON

Illustrated by
Ray Mutimer

AWARD PUBLICATIONS LIMITED

For further information on Enid Blyton please visit
www.blyton.com

ISBN 978-1-84135-485-9

This edition entitled *Mr Wumble and the Dragon and Other
Stories* published by permission of Chorion Rights Limited

First published by Award Publications Limited 2002
This edition first published 2006

Published by Award Publications Limited,
The Old Riding School, The Welbeck Estate,
Worksop, Nottinghamshire, S80 3LR

10 9 8 7 6 5 4 3 2
20 19 18 17 16 15 14 13 12 11 10 09 08

Printed in Singapore

CONTENTS

Mr Wumble and the Dragon

Mr Wumble was sitting in front of his fire, reading a book of fairytales. When he read a story about a fierce dragon with fire pouring out of his nose, he turned pale, and his hair stood up on end. When he came to where the prince rescued the princess from the fierce dragon, he cried tears of joy. Then he read how the prince married the princess and lived happily ever after, and he was so pleased that he danced a little jig round the room.

"Oh, how I wish that I could have an adventure!" cried Mr Wumble, feeling sorry for himself.

"Mr Wumble, you forget yourself!" said his parrot. He could only say three things, and that was one of them. Mrs Wumble had taught him to say them so

that when she was away, the parrot could remind Mr Wumble to behave himself.

Mr Wumble threw his spectacle case at the parrot, but it missed him and crashed into a vase that broke into more than a hundred pieces.

"Mr Wumble, I'm surprised at you," the parrot said. That was the second thing it could say.

Mr Wumble stared at the broken glass in dismay. He didn't dare to think what Mrs Wumble would say to him when she came home.

"I'm going out," said Mr Wumble,

making up his mind very quickly. "I'm going to have an adventure!"

"Have you got your handkerchief, your hat, your umbrella, your cough lozenges and your scarf?" said the parrot.

That was the third thing Mrs Wumble had taught him to say, because Mr Wumble had a bad habit of going out without putting on his hat and scarf, and coming back with a bad cold.

"Be quiet, you silly, stupid, ridiculous bird!" Mr Wumble said fiercely, putting on his hat.

"Mr Wumble, you forget yourself," said the parrot in a very haughty tone.

Mr Wumble found his handkerchief, his hat, his umbrella, and his cough lozenges. Then he tied his scarf round his neck.

"You can tell Mrs Wumble that I'm going out to look for an adventure," he said to the parrot. "I'm tired of sitting at home being poor good-for-nothing Mr Wumble! I'm going out to rescue princesses and fight fierce dragons!"

"Mr Wumble, I'm surprised at you!"

7

said the parrot. Then Mr Wumble walked out of the front door. He went out into the fields, looking for adventure as hard as he could. He looked in the hedges and in the ditches, but nothing happened at all except that his umbrella got caught in a hedge and he slipped into a ditch up to his knees.

"This is not a good day for an adventure!" Mr Wumble said to himself sadly.

Just at that very moment he caught sight of an aeroplane swooping down towards him. It looked exactly as if it was going to land on him. Mr Wumble turned and ran for his life, but he tripped over a stone and fell flat on his face.

Bump-bump-bump! The aeroplane landed just beside Mr Wumble, and someone jumped out and ran over to him.

"Have you hurt yourself?" asked the aeroplane man.

"Of course I have," Mr Wumble said crossly. "What do you want to go chasing me like that for?"

Mr Wumble stood up and looked haughtily down at the aeroplane man, who was very small with a very long nose. Mr Wumble wasn't a big man, and he felt quite pleased to be talking to someone smaller than himself for a change.

"I wasn't chasing you," the aeroplane man said humbly. "I was just going to ask you for some help."

"Well, I'm rather busy at the moment," said Mr Wumble, trying to sound important. "Busy looking for a princess to rescue or a dragon to fight, actually!"

"How marvellous!" said the aeroplane man. "I was trying to find my way to Fairyland to find a prince. There's a wretched dragon worrying the Princess of Silver River, and she sent me to find someone to rescue her. But now you can do it instead!"

"Jumping weasels!" said Mr Wumble, who often said strange things when he was surprised. Here was his adventure all right, but now he had found it, he felt a little afraid.

"Well . . . er . . . um . . . Is it a big dragon?" asked Mr Wumble, nervously.

"Enormous!" said the aeroplane man. "Hop in and I'll take you to the Princess. She will tell you the whole story."

Now Mr Wumble didn't mind going to Fairyland, but he certainly wasn't going to fight an enormous dragon. In fact, he thought that Mrs Wumble would be better at it than he would.

Still, he didn't like to seem a coward, so he said nothing more and soon found himself flying high over the town where he lived, on his way to meet the Princess of Silver River.

"But at least I am having an adventure," he said to himself. "Just wait until I tell Mrs Wumble about this!"

"Mr Wumble, I'm surprised at you," said a voice just by his ear. Mr Wumble was so astonished that he nearly fell out of the aeroplane. He turned to see who had spoken, and there was his parrot sitting on the wing of the aeroplane, scratching its head with one of its feet.

Mr Wumble looked at the parrot in dismay. "Oh, go away, you interfering, interrupting, inconvenient bird!" he said.

He gave the parrot a push, and it went over the side of the aeroplane. Mr Wumble leaned over to look where it went, and forgot to hold on to his hat, which flew away behind him.

"Drat that niggledy, naggledy, annoying bird!" he said. "It's made me lose my hat."

"Mr Wumble, you forget yourself," said a voice behind him.

Mr Wumble gave such a jump that the aeroplane wobbled from side to side. He looked round and saw the parrot was back again and, what's more, it held his hat in its feet.

"Snorting pigs!" cried Mr Wumble. "There's my hat!"

He took his hat from the parrot and put it on again, just in time for the plane to land.

"Here we are," said the aeroplane man.

The aeroplane was going downwards in circles, and when Mr Wumble looked out,

he could see a large and glittering palace just beneath them.

"Bouncing bunnies!" exclaimed Mr Wumble in great excitement. "A real, live palace!"

"Mr Wumble, you forget yourself," said the parrot. But Mr Wumble did not hear. He was far too busy feeling excited. Just think, he might soon be seeing a princess!

The aeroplane glided down on to the grass in front of the palace and came to a standstill. The little man climbed out and helped Mr Wumble down. The parrot flew on to his shoulder and wouldn't get off. Mr Wumble picked up his umbrella and felt about to make sure that he had a clean handkerchief handy.

"Now, I'm ready to see the Princess," he said.

The little man led him up some steps and came into a large, high room, where a beautiful princess lay reading on a couch. She came to meet them, and shook hands with Mr Wumble. He forgot whether he ought to bow or to curtsy, so he did both.

"And who is this?" asked the Princess, smiling so sweetly that Mr Wumble couldn't take his eyes off her.

"This is the person I've brought along to kill the dragon," explained the aeroplane man. He had taken off his baggy clothes now, and Mr Wumble saw that he was really a little gnome, with a very long, pointed nose.

14

"I see," said the Princess, smiling again. She looked so sweet that Mr Wumble decided he wouldn't tell her just yet that he wasn't going to go near any dragon, big or small.

"What's your name?" asked the Princess.

"Wumble, Your Highness – Mr Wumble," said Mr Wumble. "I am very happy to meet you."

"When would you like to go out and kill the dragon?" the Princess asked sweetly. "Before tea or after tea?"

"Er – after, I think," said Mr Wumble.

"Mr Wumble, I'm surprised at you," the parrot said loudly.

Mr Wumble went very red, for he knew he had told a story, and he was afraid that the Princess would find him out.

"What a darling, quaint bird!" said the Princess, and she actually stroked the parrot's feathers.

"I can't bear the bird myself," said Mr Wumble.

"Mr Wumble, you forget yourself," said the parrot, putting up the crest on his head very angrily.

"Oh, the pet!" cried the Princess. "Did you hear what it said?"

"I'm always hearing what it says," answered Mr Wumble.

"Here's tea," said the Princess. "I hope you're hungry. Come and sit down beside me."

Mr Wumble didn't know whether to be glad or sorry that tea had come. He wanted to eat some of the cakes that were in front of him, but he didn't like to think about the dragon he was supposed

to go out and kill directly afterwards.
The aeroplane man came over and sat
down to share the delicious tea with Mr
Wumble and the Princess.

There were six different kinds of cream
cake, two sorts of jam, and strawberry
ice cream to finish up with. Mr Wumble
didn't feel in the least like killing dragons
when he had finished.

"And now, what about the dragon?"
the Princess asked the aeroplane man.

"Perhaps you'd take Mr Wumble to the hill where it lives, Longnose?"

Longnose said he would and Mr Wumble began to feel even more uncomfortable.

"I don't like to trouble you," said Mr Wumble. "I'm sure I could go by myself if you told me where to go." Of course, Mr Wumble was hoping that he might be able to run off and hide somewhere, if only they would let him go off by himself. But they wouldn't. The Princess came with him as far as the gate, and told him she would take care of the parrot till he came back.

"And if you don't ever come back, I'll be very kind to the parrot, I promise you," she said. Mr Wumble swallowed hard.

"Have you got your handkerchief, your hat, your umbrella, your cough lozenges and your scarf?" the parrot said suddenly.

Mr Wumble felt about for his handkerchief and his cough lozenges, tied his scarf more tightly round his neck, and checked his umbrella.

"Come along, come along," said the gnome. And with the Princess waving them goodbye, they set off in search of the dragon.

"We shall soon be there," said the gnome. "I do hope you can kill this dragon. It can scorch you to a cinder if you're not careful, so you must look out for his fiery breath."

"Jumping weasels!" said Mr Wumble, feeling very shaky about the knees.

"Mr Wumble, you surprise me," said a voice, and there was the parrot flying just above them!

"Drat that meddlesome, miserable, muddling bird!" cried Mr Wumble. "I can't get rid of it!"

The parrot settled on his shoulder, and Mr Wumble had to put up with it. They all went on till they came to a hill.

"There you are," said the gnome, pointing to a column of smoke that rose in the air halfway up. "That's the dragon's breath. Come back to the palace when you've killed it."

Longnose ran down the hill and left Mr Wumble and the parrot alone. Mr Wumble turned very pale and thought he would run down the hill too. Then he thought of the Princess's smile, and suddenly he made up his mind to go and take a look at the dragon. Perhaps he could kill it somehow, but he'd have to look the other way if he did – Mr Wumble wasn't much good at killing anything.

He hadn't gone very far before he heard a most peculiar noise. It was rather like a horse's cough, but about twelve times louder. Mr Wumble stopped and listened. The noise kept on and on and on.

"Sounds like a very, very bad cough," thought Mr Wumble. "I wonder who it is."

He went on cautiously, peering round every tree to see if it was safe to go on. The noise grew louder and louder. Then he saw smoke rising above the trees.

"Snorting pigs!" said Mr Wumble in a whisper.

"Mr Wumble, you forget yourself," said

the parrot. Mr Wumble shook his fist at the parrot, and then took a look round the tree he was hiding behind.

He saw a most amazing sight. There was a big fire in the middle of a clearing, and crouched over it was a miserable-looking dragon. He was shivering from his head to his tail, and was making the strange noise that Mr Wumble had heard on his way up the hill. It was a cough – a very bad cough. Mr Wumble felt quite sorry for him.

He looked at the dragon's nose. There was no smoke coming from it – only the smouldering fire sent a blue column above the trees. Mr Wumble heaved a sigh of relief. The dragon didn't really look so terrible after all.

"Eheu, eheu, eheu!" coughed the dragon.

Mr Wumble suddenly did a strange thing. He stepped forward, held out his box of cough lozenges, and offered them to the dragon.

"Please take one," Mr Wumble said politely. "They are very good for coughs."

"Thank you," said the dragon in a hoarse tone. He put out a clawed foot, neatly took a lozenge from the box and popped it into his mouth.

"It's very good," said the dragon after a bit. "I shall be sorry to eat you after your kindness."

Mr Wumble sat down suddenly. He had been so interested in the dragon's cough that he had quite forgotten about being eaten. He felt very much upset.

"That's a nice way to repay me for my kindness," he said. "I came here to kill you, but instead I gave you a cough lozenge."

"So you did," said the dragon, generously. "Well, I won't eat you – as long as you give me all the rest of your cough lozenges."

"Well, I want some for myself," said Mr Wumble. "I get a nasty little cough in the mornings, you know."

"Give me half, then," said the dragon. "Go on, or I'll eat you up."

"You be quiet," said Mr Wumble, jumping to his feet and lunging at the

dragon with his umbrella. The dragon
gave a yell and leaped out of the way.

"Mr Wumble, I'm surprised at you,"
said the parrot, which made the dragon
look round in astonishment.

"How does that parrot know my
name?" he asked.

"Your name? Whatever do you mean?"
asked Mr Wumble, in surprise.

"My name's Wumble," answered the dragon. "Wumble the dragon. And I'm sure I heard your parrot say, 'Mr Wumble, I'm surprised at you.'"

"Well, if that isn't a funny thing!" cried Mr Wumble. "My name's Wumble too – Mr Wumble. We must be cousins or something. I can't possibly kill you now!"

"Nor can I eat you," said the dragon. "Let's sit down and have a talk instead."

So Mr Wumble and the dragon sat down by the fire and talked. They told each other all their troubles, and got on very well indeed. The dragon told Mr Wumble that he was very absent-minded, and because he was always going out without his hat and scarf, he got dreadful colds. Mr Wumble said that he was just the same.

"But at least your parrot reminds you not to be forgetful," said the dragon.

"And so does Mrs Wumble," said Mr Wumble.

"Well, what do you want a parrot for as well?" the dragon asked in astonishment.

"I don't," replied Mr Wumble, shaking

his head gloomily. "Mrs Wumble is quite enough."

"Would you give me your parrot then?" asked the dragon, eagerly. "It would be so nice to have something that called me Mr Wumble, and reminded me of all the things I forget."

Mr Wumble thought for a moment. Then he suddenly had a splendid idea.

"I'll give you my parrot and half my cough lozenges if you'll do something for me," he said.

"Oh, anything, anything," said the dragon.

"Well, look here," said Mr Wumble. "I've always wanted to be brave and splendid – but somehow I've never been able to, and Mrs Wumble scolds me dreadfully. Now, if she thought that I had really fought and conquered a dragon – don't take offence now – she would be so astonished that she probably wouldn't dare to say another cross word to me ever again. If I could get her here somehow – I expect the Princess could manage it – and you'd let me pretend to fight you, Mrs Wumble would think I was the bravest, strongest man in all the world."

"No, I don't want to," said the dragon. "I don't like the idea of you fighting me. You might get excited and forget and stick a sword into me or something."

"No, I promise I wouldn't," said Mr Wumble. "Do be a sport, Dragon. I'll give you my parrot and all my cough lozenges, if you like – but do say you will."

"Oh, all right," said the dragon. "We'll meet at the bottom of the hill tomorrow morning at ten o'clock. But you must

give me your parrot first, and the cough lozenges."

"Here you are," said Mr Wumble in delight. He handed the box to the dragon, and then placed the parrot on the dragon's shoulder. It didn't seem to mind a bit. It seemed to like the dragon much better than it had ever liked Mr Wumble. It nipped the dragon's ear very gently and spoke to him.

"Have you got your handkerchief, your hat, your umbrella, your cough lozenges and your scarf?" it said.

The dragon smiled with pleasure and said goodbye to Mr Wumble, with glad tears in his eyes.

Mr Wumble walked briskly back to the palace, feeling very pleased with himself.

When he was taken to the Princess he bowed very low and kissed her hand.

"Have you killed the dragon?" she asked in great excitement.

"No, but I have arranged that we shall have a fight tomorrow at ten o'clock," answered Mr Wumble, banging his umbrella on the ground. "I will conquer that fearsome dragon or die in the attempt."

"Oh, you brave man!" said the Princess. "What do you ask in return for all this?"

"I ask that my wife, Mrs Wumble, may be fetched here to see the fight," said Mr Wumble.

"But don't you want a palace or anything as well?" asked the Princess, in surprise. "We usually give a palace, or a castle, and bags of gold to people who kill dragons."

"Oh, well, I'd like a palace," said Mr Wumble. "And a few bags of gold would come in useful."

"Very well," said the Princess. "It shall be done."

Mr Wumble was so excited that he hardly knew what to do. To think that he, ordinary Mr Wumble, was having an adventure with a Princess, a dragon, bags of gold, and a palace, all mixed up together!

At half past nine the next morning Mr Wumble watched the aeroplane go off to fetch Mrs Wumble. At five minutes to ten it was back again. Mrs Wumble climbed out of the aeroplane and stared round at everybody.

"Where's Mr Wumble?" she said in a stern voice. "He broke one of my best vases yesterday, and I want to ask him how he did it."

"Oh, you can't ask him now," said the Princess. "He's getting ready to fight a dragon. See, he's putting on his armour, and trying his sword and shield."

Mrs Wumble looked. She could hardly believe her eyes.

Mr Wumble was feeling tremendously excited. The gnome had brought him some shining armour to put on, and he was having a lovely time strutting up and down, waving his sword in the air, and shouting fiercely and loudly in a voice that Mrs Wumble had never heard him use before.

Just at that moment a roaring noise was heard from the hill, and everyone trembled. It was the dragon!

"Do not fear!" shouted Mr Wumble loudly.

Another tremendous roar came from the hillside, and a puff of smoke went up in the air.

"He is breathing out fire and smoke!" cried everybody in terror.

"I will protect you all," shouted Mr Wumble, even louder.

"Oh, isn't he brave!" said the Princess to Mrs Wumble.

Suddenly the dragon leaped into sight, gnashing his teeth so that they sounded like crashing rocks.

Mr Wumble felt a bit nervous. The dragon was looking very fierce, and Mr Wumble hoped the dragon wouldn't forget he was only pretending.

The dragon roared again and jumped up very high in the air. Mr Wumble thought the dragon was overdoing things.

"I ought to have given him the cough lozenges afterwards, not before," he thought. "He may think that I would make a nice breakfast and forget all about my kindness yesterday. Well, if I'm going to be eaten, I might as well give the dragon a few jabs first."

Mr Wumble dashed forward and lunged at the dragon with his sword. He leaped about, shouting and lunging all the time, keeping out of the way of the dragon's mouth as well as he could.

The dragon dodged about, and kept jumping high into the air, which was very annoying. Mr Wumble jabbed at the dragon once as it came down just

34

beside him, and pricked him.

"Ow!" yelled the dragon. Then he turned round and put his mouth close to Mr Wumble's ear.

"If you do that again I'll eat you!" he whispered fiercely. "I thought we were only going to pretend to fight."

"Sorry," said Mr Wumble, glad that the dragon was pretending after all. "Come on, let's dodge round each other again."

Off they went again, while the watching people cheered and shouted, groaned and clapped as loudly as ever they could. Mr Wumble danced round and round the dragon, waving his sword merrily, and thoroughly enjoying himself. The dragon lashed about and roared fiercely, but neither of them hurt each other at all. Then suddenly the dragon knocked Mr Wumble flat on the ground with his tail by mistake.

"If you do that again I'll jab my sword into your tail, hard!" Mr Wumble said fiercely, getting to his feet.

"Very sorry," said the dragon. "Let's finish now, shall we? I feel as if I want to go and take another of those cough lozenges."

"Come on, then," said Mr Wumble, and he shouted so loudly that the dragon jumped. They pretended to go for each other more fiercely than ever, and at last

the dragon rolled over with a dreadful groan, and lay stretched out on the ground.

"Go, fearful beast, before I kill you!" shouted Mr Wumble, loud enough for everyone to hear. "Go back to your home far, far away, and never come to this land again."

At once the dragon got up and galloped away at a great pace, groaning as it went. It went on and on and on, until it could be seen no more.

"I hope my cough lozenges will really cure his cough," thought Mr Wumble to himself. He had fancied he heard it coughing as it ran away. Then he heard everybody cheering loudly, and Mrs Wumble flung her arms round his neck.

"Oh, my brave, brave Wumble!" she cried. "I'm so proud of you. I won't say a word about that vase you broke!"

"I should think not!" said Mr Wumble in a stern voice. "I hope you will never dare to grumble at me for a stupid thing like that, Mrs Wumble, when I have been busy killing a dragon!"

He went back to the Princess, and she kissed him lightly on both cheeks, and they all went to the palace for a grand feast. Mr Wumble sat with Mrs Wumble and the Princess at the head of the table, and was very happy. He kept his armour on, because he felt so grand in it, but it was very difficult to get his handkerchief out, so he had to take it off after a bit.

"And now about your palace?" said the Princess. "When would you like it?"

Mrs Wumble's eyes nearly fell out of her head.

"Oh, any time," said Mr Wumble in a sort of don't-care voice.

"Oh, Mr Wumble, do let's have it now!" begged Mrs Wumble.

"Oh, very well, I'll have it now," said Mr Wumble. "And a few bags of gold, Your Highness, if it's all the same to you."

The princess turned to her butler.

"See that everything's ready for Mr Wumble as soon as you can," she said. The butler bowed and went out.

After the meal was over, Mr and Mrs Wumble were taken to see their palace. It stood on the hill where the dragon had been, and was very grand indeed. Mr Wumble was delighted. He said goodbye to the Princess, and then, taking Mrs Wumble's hand, he led her into the palace.

"Oh, you brave, brave man!" cried Mrs

Wumble again, and kissed him on his nose. Mr Wumble smiled all over his face. He was the happiest man in the world, and there was only one thing he wished – he would very much have liked to have the dragon for a pet.

"He was such a nice, sensible beast," thought Mr Wumble. "But, still, it would never have done. I only hope he's happy where he is, and has got rid of that nasty cough! As for the parrot, good riddance to bad rubbish, I say!"

Then Mr and Mrs Wumble settled down in their new palace, and you will be glad to know that, even though they were not a prince and princess, they lived happily ever after.

When Mother
Lost Her Purse

There was a circus in the village. Betty and Jack had seen the caravans and trucks coming along the road. They had even seen a clown turning head-over-heels in the road. "And once he went splash in a puddle!" said Betty, laughing as she told her mother all she had seen. "Wouldn't it be lovely if we could go and see him at the circus. I would so love to."

"Oh, Mum, can we?" asked Jack. "Do, do take us. We've been ever so good this week, haven't we?"

"Yes, you have," answered Mother, smiling. "Well, I'll take you both this evening!"

"Oh! Oh! Oh! How lovely!" cried Jack and Betty, dancing round in delight.

"We'll see the jugglers!" shouted Jack.

"And the clown!" cried Betty.

Mother laughed. "Yes, it will be great fun!" she said. "Run off to school now, dears, or you'll be late."

Jack and Betty went off to school, and told everyone that they were going to the circus that evening.

They rushed home to tea as fast as their legs could carry them, and burst into the house like runaway ponies.

"Mummy! Mummy!" they cried. "How long is it till we go to the circus?"

Their mother was in the kitchen, taking some hot currant buns out of the oven. She turned to smile, but her eyes looked sorrowful.

"My dears," she said, "I've got a terrible disappointment for you. We can't go to the circus after all."

"Oh, Mum! Why ever not?" asked Jack in dismay.

"I've lost my purse," said Mother, sadly. "I went out shopping this afternoon, and when I got home I couldn't find my purse. I must have dropped it in the road, but when I went to look for it, I couldn't find it anywhere."

"Was there a lot of money in it?" asked Jack.

"Yes," said Mother. "And now that I've lost it, I can't afford to take you to the circus, you see. I'm dreadfully sorry, my dears."

"Poor old Mum," said Jack, putting his arm round her. "Never mind. We don't mind."

But Betty began to cry. "*I* mind," she sobbed. "Haven't you got some other money somewhere to take us with, Mummy?" she asked. "You did promise, you know."

"Be quiet, Betty," said Jack. "We aren't

babies any more, to cry over a little disappointment."

"It isn't a little disappointment, it's a big one," answered Betty, truthfully. But she dried her eyes. If Jack was going to be brave, she was too.

"I've made you some lovely hot currant buns for tea," said Mother, kissing Betty. "Let's all try hard and forget our disappointment and be really brave about it. We're none of us babies, are we?"

"No, we're not!" said Jack. "Cheer up, Betty. Let's go out and play a game in the garden before tea."

"You've got just half an hour," said their mother. "I wonder if you'd mind sweeping up some of those fallen leaves in the front garden for me? I noticed how terribly untidy they were when I came in earlier."

"Come on, Betty, we'll go and tidy them all up!" cried Jack, trying to be cheerful. He took hold of Betty's arm and pulled her out of doors.

"I don't feel like doing anything like that," said Betty, miserably.

"Nor do I," said Jack. "But think how poor Mum must feel. She's just as disappointed as we are, so let's do something to cheer her up. I know she'd be pleased to see the front garden nice and tidy."

"All right," said Betty, trying to smile. "I'll go and get the wheelbarrow, Jack. You fetch the brooms."

Soon both children were busy. Jack swept the leaves into big heaps and Betty lifted them into the wheelbarrow. When it was full, they wheeled it over to the rubbish-heap and emptied it.

It was very hard work, but neither of
the children was lazy. They had filled
and emptied the barrow twice, and were
filling it a third time when something
fell with a loud thud against the side of
the barrow, just as Betty threw in a pile
of crackly leaves.

"You've found a chestnut!" said Jack.
"Look and see. It might be a good one.
The wind has blown lots down among
the leaves."

Betty looked but she could not see anything. She put her hand in among the dry, crackly leaves and felt about.

"I can't feel anything," she was beginning to say, when suddenly her hand closed on something that felt quite hard.

She pulled it out and looked at it. It wasn't a chestnut. Oh no! It was something much better than that.

"Jack! Jack!" squeaked Betty, so suddenly that Jack dropped his broom in fright. "Look! It's Mummy's purse! And it's still full of money!"

"Hurrah! Hurrah!" shouted Jack. "She must have dropped it in the garden and the piles of leaves hid it. Hurrah!"

"Come in and tell Mummy!" cried Betty, too excited to stand still. She and Jack ran into the house, shouting at the tops of their voices.

"Goodness gracious!" said Mother in alarm. "Whatever is the matter?"

"Your purse, your purse!" shouted the children. "We found it in the leaves!"

"Oh, how lovely!" said their mother, taking her purse and opening it. "And all the money is safe. We can go to the circus, after all!"

"It's too good to be true!" said Jack, bursting with delight.

"And just think, my dears," said Mother suddenly, "if you hadn't been brave and unselfish over your disappointment, you wouldn't have found my purse!"

"But we have found it; we *have* found it!" cried Betty. "Let's hurry up and have tea and go!"

And very soon off they went to the

circus. They had the most wonderful time watching the acrobats and jugglers. The clowns made them laugh so hard that they thought their sides would burst. They clappped and cheered and wished that the circus could last for ever. But at last it came to an end and it was time for them to go home to bed.

"Thank you, my dears. If you had not found my purse we would all have missed the fun," answered Mother.

They chattered brightly all the way home and they all agreed it was the very nicest circus in the world. And I really think they deserved it, don't you?

Tit
for Tat

Jennifer, the curly-haired doll, had a little hairbrush of her own. She was very proud of it indeed, and the toys liked it too, because it was fun to brush out Jennifer's lovely golden curls at night. Sometimes she lent it to the toys. Then the teddy bear brushed his short fur, the black dog brushed his mop of black hair, the pink cat brushed his coat and the clockwork mouse brushed his whiskers.

The little hairbrush lived in a small box. Sally, the little girl who owned all the toys, never bothered with it at all. She hadn't brushed Jennifer's hair once with it, so it was a good thing the toys took turns at brushing her hair to make it look nice.

Then one day a most annoying thing

happened. Sally was cleaning out her doll's-house and she wanted a brush to sweep the little carpets. She didn't want to borrow her mother's brush because it was much too big for the tiny carpets. So can you guess what she did? She used Jennifer's little hairbrush. Just the thing!

"It's just right for this job," said Sally, brushing away at the carpet. "What a good thing I thought of it."

But the toys didn't think so at all! They looked on in dismay and Jennifer was almost in tears. Her own little hairbrush! How mean of Sally!

"Now I shan't be able to brush my hair with it any more," she thought. "It will be dirty and horrid. I do wish Sally had used something else. It's too bad of her."

Sally finished brushing the carpets and looked at the little brush. Such hard sweeping had almost worn it out. "It's no use now," she said. "I'll throw it away." And into the rubbish bin it went! Oh dear!

Jennifer cried that night. "I did like my little hairbrush," she said. "I've got such a lot of hair that I need a brush for it. Sally never brushes it for me. She doesn't look as if she brushes her own hair, either."

"She's an untidy little girl," said the bear. "She doesn't brush her teeth either. But she tells her mother that she does. She's a naughty story-teller."

"Yes, she is," said the pink cat. "Her mother gave her a nice new green toothbrush last week and Sally hasn't used it yet! She hasn't cleaned her teeth all week."

"Then a toothbrush is just wasted on

her!" said the clockwork mouse. "It's a pity we can't take it and use it to brush Jennifer's hair each night!"

"That's a very fine idea, Mouse!" said the bear. "However did you think of it?"

The clockwork mouse would have blushed with delight at this praise if he could. "I don't know how I thought of it," he said. "I must be cleverer than I imagined."

"Shall we get Sally's toothbrush then?" said the pink cat. "I could climb up to the basin in the bathroom and reach up for it, I think. It's in her mug."

"All right. You go then," said the bear, and the pink cat went. He was quite good at jumping. He leaped up to the basin, climbed up on to the shelf above, took Sally's perfectly new toothbrush in his mouth and jumped down to the floor again.

He padded into the playroom with it. The toys looked at it.

"The handle's too long," said the bear. "Much too long."

"Cut a bit off then," said the pink cat.

"Sally's got some tools in a box," said Jennifer, the doll. "There's a little saw there. We could use that."

They found the little saw, and the bear sawed away at the handle of the toothbrush. Everyone watched in excitement. The end of the handle suddenly fell off. The mouse picked up the little brush in delight. "Its handle is

nice and short now," he said. "Just right for a hairbrush. Jennifer, do let me brush your hair for you."

So he was the first to brush the doll's curly hair with the new brush. It brushed beautifully because it had harder bristles than the hairbrush. Jennifer was delighted.

"Where shall we keep this brush?" asked the bear. "Better not put it into the box because Sally might see it."

"Put it into me," said the little teapot, in a spouty voice. "Sally never plays with me now. She'll never look inside me."

So that is where the toys keep the new

hairbrush. The bear was a little bit worried at first. "Do you think we've done wrong to use Sally's toothbrush?" he said.

"Well, Sally took my brush and now we've taken hers, so it's tit for tat," said the doll. "Anyway, she never used her toothbrush! We wouldn't have taken it if she did."

I'm just wondering what is going to happen when Sally's mother discovers that Sally's toothbrush is gone. It's going to be very difficult for naughty little Sally to make her mother believe that she is cleaning her teeth each night with a toothbrush that isn't there!

Binkle's
Tail

Once there was a guinea-pig called
Binkle. He lived in a cage just outside
Jinky the gnome's front door, and he was
very proud of himself.

"My whiskers are fine, my fur is soft,
and my ears are pretty!" he said to
himself. "No wonder all Jinky's visitors
come and talk to me!"

But one day Panikin the pixie said
something that gave Binkle a terrible
fright.

"Whatever you do, Jinky, don't let
anyone hold Binkle up by his tail. If
you do, his eyes will fall out!" he said
solemnly.

"Oh! Oh! Oh!" squeaked poor Binkle,
hiding himself in a corner. "I do hope
nobody would do such a cruel thing!"

Jinky the gnome and Panikin the pixie laughed loudly and Binkle couldn't think what they were laughing at. When they had gone, he began thinking very hard.

"Just suppose someone did come and hold me up by my tail!" he thought. "How terrible it would be! I wonder what my tail is like?" He tried to see it, but he was such a plump little guinea-pig that he couldn't see anything beyond his humpy back.

"It must be rather a long tail," he said sadly. "Perhaps Panikin was afraid some rude person would swing me upside down by it. Oh dear! What shall I do?"

The more he thought about it, the more he felt afraid. At last he decided to run away that night, go to Snip the tailor, and ask him to cut his tail right off. "Then no one can hold me up by it!" thought Binkle.

So that night, out he scampered, and ran down the road to Snip the tailor.

Snip was sitting making a coat for a brownie. "Hello!" he said in surprise. "What do you want, Binkle?"

"Please would you cut my tail off?" begged Binkle. "I'm afraid someone will hold me up by it, and then my eyes would drop out, you know."

Snip stared at him, and smiled. "I'm terribly sorry," he said, "but I'm afraid my scissors couldn't cut off your tail, they're not the right sort. Go and ask Periwinkle the dressmaker. She's got a pair of brand-new scissors!"

"Thank you," said Binkle and off he

scampered. As he went he heard Snip laughing, and he couldn't think what he was laughing at. He climbed the hill to Periwinkle's.

"I want my tail cut off, in case someone holds me up by it and makes my eyes fall out," explained Binkle. "Snip said you'd got a new pair of scissors."

"So I have. But I'm afraid they wouldn't cut your tail off, Binkle," said Periwinkle. "Go and ask Pippit the draper. He's got lots of scissors there."

"Thank you," said Binkle, and ran off as quickly as he could. As he went, he heard Periwinkle laughing, and he couldn't think what she was laughing at.

Pippit the draper was just shutting up shop when Binkle came panting up.

"Why, Binkle!" said Pippit. "Why are you out so late?"

"I'm dreadfully worried about my tail," said Binkle. "If I'm held up by it, my eyes will drop out. Periwinkle said you could cut it off, as you have lots of scissors."

"So I have," said Pippit, laughing. "But they're all much too small. Why don't you go to the Simple Witch down in the valley? She's got a pair of magic scissors."

Binkle hurried to the witch's cottage, wondering why Pippit had laughed, and asked for her help. "Pippit said you had some magic scissors. It won't hurt, will it?"

"Oh no, Binkle, it won't hurt you at all!" chuckled the Simple Witch.

She picked up a pair of big, shiny

scissors. Binkle turned his back to her and waited nervously. *Snip! Snap!* he heard, but he felt nothing at all.

"There you are!" said the witch. "You haven't any tail to worry about now, Binkle!"

"Oh, thank you very much indeed!" said Binkle, and ran home, full of delight.

As he went, he heard the witch laughing and laughing, and he couldn't think what she was laughing at. He cuddled himself up in his little cage, and felt very happy.

"Now I'm quite safe," he thought. "My eyes will never drop out. I wonder what Jinky will say. Won't he be pleased to think no one can ever hold me up by my tail!"

Binkle soon fell fast asleep. When he woke next day he tried to look over his plump shoulder to check that his tail wasn't there. But, of course, he was much too fat.

Just then, Jinky came whistling down the garden. But, dear me, he didn't seem to notice anything new about Binkle at all, and he couldn't think why the little guinea-pig kept turning his back on him. "What's the matter, Binkle?" he asked at last.

"I've had my tail cut off," said Binkle proudly, "so that no one can hold me up

by it and make my eyes fall out! The
Simple Witch did it with her magic
scissors!"

To his surprise, Jinky began to laugh
and laugh, and Binkle couldn't think
what he was laughing at. "What's the
matter?" he asked, quite offended.

"Oh, Binkle – hee, hee, hee – it's so
funny – ha, ha – you never had a tail at
all – ho, ho, ho! Guinea-pigs don't have
tails, you silly!" Jinky said, laughing
loudly.

And then Binkle knew why Snip and Periwinkle, Pippit and the Simple Witch had all laughed so loudly the night before. Poor Binkle!

The Bright
Little Pound

Mary and John had such a nice surprise one morning. Mother told them that Uncle Jack had been to see her the night before, when they were in bed – and had left a bright new pound coin for the two children!

How pleased they were!

"Oh, Mummy, Robert and Jean are coming to tea today!" said Mary. "Can we spend the money on some cakes? You said you wouldn't have time to make any for us today."

"You can spend it how you like," said Mother, smiling. "The baker should be coming soon. You can go and keep a good look out for him."

So Mary and John ran out of doors and swung on the gate, looking for the baker's van. They knew it quite well. It was bright blue. They often saw it going down the road.

"Look!" said John. "There's the mail van outside the post office! I expect there are a lot of parcels and letters today!"

As he spoke, a postman came out with two large sacks. He threw them onto the red mail van and then went back for some more. Another postman came out of the post office with a sack – but he did not go to the mail van, he walked down the street. He had some letters to deliver to people's houses.

Soon the children heard *rat-a-tat-tat* all the way down the road. It was fun watching the postman going to the different houses. Once he had to stop until the door was opened, because there was a parcel to hand in.

"Here's the baker's van!" said Mary at last. "I can see it coming up the road! Hurrah! Now we can choose our cakes! Don't let's wait till the baker gets here, John. Let's go and buy them right now!"

The children scampered down the road

to the baker. He had opened his van at the back, and was taking out a tray.

"Baker, baker, have you any nice cakes today?" asked Mary, running up. "We have some money to spend, and we want to buy some cakes for tea."

"I have some nice currant buns," said the baker. He took out a tray of cakes and buns and showed them to the children.

"Oh, we'll have two buns, please," said John. "I love buns. They look nice, sticky ones, too!"

"That's twenty pence," said the baker. "Is there anything else you would like?"

"How much are these sugary cakes?" asked Mary, pointing to some iced cakes with jam in them. "They look lovely."

"They are four for sixty pence," said the baker. "There are some pink ones and some white ones. Would you like two pink and two white?"

"Oh yes," said John. So the baker put the two buns and the four iced cakes into a bag and gave it to the children. How pleased they were! They gave him their pound coin.

"There's twenty pence change," said the baker. "Twenty pence for the buns, and sixty pence for the cakes makes eighty – twenty pence change!"

The children said thank you, and ran home with their cakes.

"What shall we do with the change?" asked Mary.

"I know!" said John. "We'll write a postcard to thank Uncle Jack for the pound and we will buy a stamp with the last twenty pence!"

"Good idea!" said Mary. "I'll get one of my postcards now."

So she got one that she had painted herself, and together the children made up what to write.

> *Dear Uncle Jack,*
> *Thank you for your nice new pound coin. We have bought two buns and four cakes with it, and we are buying a stamp for this postcard.*
> *Love from Mary and John.*

Mother said it was written very nicely.

She said they could go to the post office and buy a stamp and post the card themselves. So off they went.

"I'll buy the stamp and you can post the card," said John. So they went into the big post office, and pushed their money over the counter. The girl gave them a stamp. John stuck it on the card. They went out and Mary ran to the letterbox. She posted the card and both children heard it go *plop*! It was safely in the box! The postman would take it out and another postman would deliver it to Uncle Jack.

"What fun we've had with that pound coin!" said Mary. "Two buns, four cakes and a stamp! The baker and the postman have worked hard for us today. What would we do without them!"

All The Way to
Santa Claus

It was nearly Christmas time, and Santa Claus and all his helpers were very busy making thousands of toys in the workshop below Santa's castle.

Tops were humming, rocking-horses were rocking, trains were rattling round and round on their rails, and teddy bears were practising their growls. The toy-makers were working very hard, and everywhere you went there were toys being made, ready for Christmas.

Now one of the little workers was a brownie called Slick. He was the one that taught the jacks-in-the-boxes to pop up on their springs and make people jump. Nobody liked him very much. He didn't always tell the truth, and what he liked doing best was to play tricks on people.

"I don't trust him," said one brownie to another. "And I wish he would go away." But Santa Claus overheard and told the brownies not to be nasty. Little did Santa know that Slick was planning a very nasty trick indeed. He had decided to steal the sack of toys that Santa Claus was going to take out with him on Christmas Eve!

Now, this sack was a magic sack. It looked as if it could hold only a hundred toys, but it could really hold as many toys as Santa needed to give away on Christmas Eve!

Slick had asked Mr Hessian, who made a new sack for Santa every year, how he managed to fit all the toys into one sack.

"It's easy!" said Mr Hessian, who was busy sewing some magic into every stitch. "On Christmas Eve Santa blows a whistle, and all the toys come to life. Then they march out of their different toy-rooms in a long line, and walk straight into the sack. It doesn't matter how many there are, they can all fit in. Then Santa Claus ties up the neck of the

sack, and goes off with it in his sledge."

That was all that Slick wanted to know. Now he knew just what to do!

"I'll pretend that there is to be a practice march into the sack this year," he said to himself. "And I'll be the one to blow the whistle and hold the sack open for the toys to march in! Then I'll tie it up and use one of the toy cars to take me to the Land of Boys and Girls. I'll sell the toys to all the toyshops there and make a lot of money! What a splendid trick that will be!"

So, one night when all the other

brownies were asleep, Slick told all the toys that there was to be a practice march into the sack.

"When I blow my whistle, you must all come quickly," he said.

He blew his whistle and at once the teddy bears got up and marched, growling, into the sack. The ducks waddled and quacked, and the dolls walked in. The trains rushed in at top speed and so did the toy cars. The balls rolled along, the tops spun there, and even the bricks hopped, skipped or jumped along. As for the toy soldiers, they marched smartly in a line behind their captain. It really was a sight to see.

"It's only a practice march," whispered the dolls. "We shan't be in this smelly sack very long!"

But, to their great dismay, Slick tightly tied up the neck of the sack and began to drag it along the floor to the back door, where he had his car waiting! Nobody heard the toys crying out for help. It really was very easy for Slick to steal them all.

In two minutes the big castle was quiet again. No growling, clattering, rocking, or quacking disturbed the silence, for not a toy was left. They were all crowded together in the magic sack, being driven off to be sold in toyshops in the Land of Boys and Girls.

The captain of the soldiers soon guessed that something was wrong. He shouted out to Slick.

"Hey! What are you doing with us? Where are you taking us? Let us out! I shall complain to Santa Claus!"

Slick laughed loudly. "You'll never see him again. Just imagine what the children will say when they find out that Santa Claus hasn't any toys to give them for Christmas!"

The toys were frightened and upset. They all began to talk at once and the tops hummed so loudly that it was difficult to hear what was being said.

"Silence!" shouted the captain of the toy soldiers. "I have a plan. Please listen carefully, all of you."

When the toys stopped making a noise,

the captain spoke in a quiet voice.

"We need to find our way back to Santa Claus as soon as possible," he said. "It is nearly Christmas Eve and if we don't return, there will be no presents for Santa to take to the children. I have a sharp sword, and I am going to cut a hole in the side of the sack. My soldiers and I will escape through the hole. Once we are out, you must follow us and we will lead you back to the castle!"

Then, taking his sharp sword, the brave captain cut a large hole in the sack.

Out he marched with his soldiers close behind, and they found themselves at the back of the car. It was not going very

fast, because there was snow on the ground, and Slick was driving very slowly in case he skidded.

One by one the soldiers climbed out of the car, and silently dropped down on to the snowy ground. All the toys followed them as quietly as they could. Soon the sack was quite empty but Slick didn't know that. Oh, no! He drove on, thinking that he still had hundreds of toys behind him!

The toys looked around them. It was evening and they were on the outskirts of a big town. They wondered what they should do next.

"There's a policeman!" whispered a big doll. "Shall we ask him the way back to Santa Claus?"

So the toys made their way in a long line, over the snow, to the policeman. But when he saw this strange collection of tiny things moving towards him, he thought he must be seeing things and ran away back to the police station.

"He's run away," said the captain, crossly. "Now what shall we do?"

80

Just then one of the teddy bears cried out, "Look – there's somebody else coming up the road – two people. Oh, they're children!"

Sure enough, two children were trudging along in the snowy night. The soldiers followed their captain to a lamppost, and there the children saw them, a long line of little shining toys.

"Look, Sophie – toy soldiers – and oh, my goodness, there are dolls too – and toy bears and pandas – lots of them. Are we dreaming?"

"We must be, James," said Sophie. "But it's a lovely dream. Listen – this little soldier is speaking to us!"

"Do you know the way to Santa's castle?" the captain was asking, in a high, squeaky voice. "Somebody stole us away from there tonight, and we want to go back."

Well, of course Sophie and James made the same answer that you would have made.

"We don't know! We know he lives in a castle somewhere in a snowy land where reindeer live, but we couldn't possibly tell you the way!"

"Oh, dear! What are we going to do? We really must get back!" said a big doll. "It's almost Christmas time and we're the toys that Santa Claus puts into children's stockings! We're not shop toys, you know."

"Perhaps a reindeer could tell us the way," said the captain. "All reindeer know the way to the land of Santa Claus. Do you have a pet reindeer that we could ask?"

"No!" said Sophie, with a laugh. "But there are reindeer at the zoo, and that's not very far from here."

"Could you please take us there?" asked the captain. "Maybe the reindeer can help us find the way."

"The zoo is closed now," said James. "But we could take you to the gates, and as you are so small you could easily slip through the railings."

"I don't know how to thank you," said the captain. "I shall tell Santa Claus all about you when we get back, and I will ask him to bring you some special toys this Christmas, as a reward for your help."

"What are your names?" asked the big doll, as they all walked down the street through the snow.

"I'm James and my sister is Sophie," said James. "This is a funny thing to happen! I still wonder if I'm dreaming!"

After some time they came to the gates of the big zoo, and the toys slipped through the railings. They called goodbye to Sophie and James and went into the dark zoo. They heard a wolf howling, and they heard owls hooting. And then they smelled the familiar smell of reindeer! The captain sniffed hard.

"I can smell them," he said. "Their house must be somewhere near here. Come along."

So, through the zoo, along the snowy paths, went a long, long line of toys, much to the surprise of the zoo animals.

At last the toys came to the reindeer house. The reindeer were fast asleep. There were two of them, and the captain

gently prodded them until they woke up
with a jump.

"Who's that?" said one reindeer.

"Excuse me please, reindeer, but do
you know where Santa Claus lives?"
asked the captain.

"Of course," said the reindeer. "I used
to live not far from his castle. I always
hoped I'd be chosen to draw his sledge

at Christmas, but I never was. I even practised galloping through the sky, like his sledge reindeer do. But I wasn't fast enough. Why do you want to know?"

"Well, we are all Christmas toys, and somebody stole us from Santa Claus's castle," said the captain. "But we escaped. And now we want to go back. Could you please, please, tell us the way?"

"Well, you want to go the sky-way – it's much quicker than any other way," said the reindeer. "Can you see that big star there? Well, you go straight towards

that, but at midnight you steer by those three stars to the right . . . and . . ."

The listening toys groaned. None of them knew how to fly through the sky. But just at that moment one of the teddy bears had a brilliant idea.

"Reindeer, you know how to gallop through the air, don't you? Could you possibly take us on your back, do you think? Santa Claus would be so grateful to you."

"What a good idea!" said the first reindeer, beginning to get excited. And soon the two of them had agreed to help the toys.

First the reindeer had to remember the spell that was used for galloping in the sky. Then they decided that it would be wise to practise for a bit first, for neither of them had flown for many years. As they uttered the magic words, the reindeer began to rise up and up into the air, while the toys watched from below.

They flew round and round practising, and it wasn't long before they felt confident enough to land and pick up the toys. One of the zoo keepers looked up and saw the reindeer in the sky, but he didn't believe what he was seeing.

"There must be something wrong with my eyes," he said, shaking his head. "Reindeer in the sky, indeed! Why, I'll be believing in Santa Claus next!" Chuckling, he went back into his office and didn't do anything about them at all, which was a very good thing.

Gently the reindeer glided to a halt in front of the toys.

"All aboard," they said and the toys climbed on to the reindeers' backs – and not only on to their backs, but on their necks and noses and even their tails! There were so very many toys, you see.

They all managed to get on at last, and then – off they went! It was so exciting to be galloping through the sky.

The toys had to hang on tightly because the reindeer went so fast. They flew high over snow-covered fields and villages and at last they arrived at the castle of Santa Claus. The reindeer

stamped up the steps puffing and
blowing and feeling very important.

The castle door opened and down the
steps came Santa Claus. All his workers
followed him looking very surprised.
They were so pleased to see that all the
toys had come back.

"Where have you been, toys?" cried Santa Claus. "And who are these fine reindeer?"

The toys crowded round Santa, all trying to speak at once.

"Shh," said Santa, laughing. "One at a time. I can't understand what you are saying."

The captain of the toy soldiers stepped forward and told Santa Claus all about their adventure. There was such an excited humming and squeaking and growling all around that Santa Claus could hardly hear.

"That naughty Slick!" he cried. "But he'll be sorry when he realises that he's stuck in the Land of Boys and Girls. I shall only let him back when he's mended his wicked ways. Now I must reward Sophie and James, and these two reindeer. What reward would you like?"

"Oh, please Santa Claus, may we help to draw your sledge on Christmas Eve?" asked the reindeer. "We could gallop here from the zoo."

"All right!" said Santa Claus. "Come

along here on Christmas Eve at eight o'clock, so that I can get you ready. And now – what about these children, Sophie and James? I'd better take them some extra-special presents, I think. Where do they live, Captain?"

Well, would you believe it, nobody knew!

"I forgot to ask for their address," said the captain. "And I don't know their surnames, either. Oh dear, how will you reward Sophie and James now, Santa Claus?"

"I'll have to look in my special Christmas book for all the children named Sophie and James," said Santa Claus, "and I'll leave all of them some extra-special toys. That's the only thing I can do! Now come along to bed, all of you. You must be very tired."

Well, that is the story of how all the Christmas toys were stolen, and how they got back safely to Santa Claus. I hope your name is Sophie or James, because if it is, you'll be very lucky this year, won't you?

The
Lost Beads

When Angela, the big doll, lost her beads, she was really upset. She went crying to the toys, and they all listened to her story.

"I was walking in the garden when my necklace suddenly broke," said Angela, weeping. "And nearly all the beads rolled away down a hole. I put my hand down but I couldn't reach them. Look, I've only got two blue beads left of my lovely necklace."

"Don't cry, Angela," said the teddy bear. "We'll get Pip along – he's a pixie who likes toys, you know – and Jinky too. They'll think of something to get back your beads!"

So Pip and Jinky were fetched, and they thought of something at once, of course!

"Down that hole, did you say?" said Pip. "Now let me see . . . no good asking the rabbit for help – he'd scrape too big a hole and scatter the beads everywhere. I know, we'll get the mole. Go and fetch him, Jinky."

Well, before long, a curious little hillock of earth appeared in the garden – and out of the top of it came the mole's sharp little snout. "What would you like me to do?" he asked.

Pip told him. "See that hole nearby, Mole? Well, Angela's beads are there. Burrow a hole to them, will you, and collect them for her? You're always burrowing after beetles and grubs – why not burrow after beads for a change?"

"Right," said the mole, "I will," and disappeared underground again. They heard a lot of tunnelling going on, and then he popped up again. "Can't talk very well," he mumbled. "Got my mouth full of beads. Here they are!"

Angela was so pleased. She promised to tell him the very next time she saw a fat slug that would do for his dinner. "He's clever, isn't he?" she said to Pip. "And so are you! Thank you very much!"

The Little Bear's Adventure

Once upon a time there was a little brown bear. He lived on the top shelf in the toyshop, with his best friend, a duck. They had been there for a whole year. Fancy that! A whole year!

They were very unhappy about it. They got dustier and dustier, and had almost given up hope of ever being sold. They longed to have a little boy or girl to own them.

You see, by some mistake, the duck had a bear's growl and the bear had a duck's quack. It was most upsetting. Whenever the bear was squeezed in his middle, he said "Quack!" very loudly indeed – and whenever the duck was squeezed she said "Grr-rrr!"

The shopkeeper had tried to sell them,

but she couldn't, and so she had put them away on the top shelf.

One day a little girl came into the shop with her mother. She had come to spend the money that her granny had given her for her birthday.

"I want a bear and a duck," she said. Then she pointed up to the shelf. "Oh, look!" she said. "There's a lovely little brown bear, and he has a duck right next to him."

The shopkeeper took them down – how excited the bear and duck felt when they thought they might be sold to this nice little girl!

"Do they say anything?" she asked.

"Well," said the shopkeeper, "it's rather funny. The bear quacks like a duck, and the duck growls like a bear. A mistake was made, and it is impossible to put it right."

The little girl pressed the bear and he made a loud quack. Then she pressed the duck and of course she had to growl – "Grr-rrr!"

"Oh," said the little girl, disappointed, "what a pity! They make the wrong sounds. I'm afraid I don't want them."

The little bear was quite upset. He put a comforting paw on duck's shoulder. The little girl looked at them again, and they looked so sad that she felt quite sorry for them.

"I'd like to get a bear that growls properly and a duck that quacks in the right way," she said. "But if I can't I might come back and buy these two."

"Very well," said the shopkeeper, and she put the two toys back on the top shelf again. They watched the little girl go out of the shop. They felt most unhappy. To think they could have gone to live with a nice girl like that.

That night the bear spoke to the duck. "Quack!" he said. "Duck, listen to me. It's quite time we did something to help ourselves."

"Grr-rrr!" said the duck.

"We will go to the Little Wise Woman on the hill," said the bear, "and ask for her help. Maybe she can do something for us." He jumped down from the shelf, went over to a window which was open at the bottom, and jumped through.

"Come on, Duck," he called, and the duck waddled out behind him across the wet grass.

After a long walk, they came to the hill where the Little Wise Woman lived. Her cottage was at the top, and the two toys could see that it was brightly lit.

The Little Wise Woman was having a party, but just as the two toys approached, the guests began to leave. Out went Dame Big-Feet the witch, on her broomstick. Out went Mrs Twinkle, the plump, jolly woman who sold balloons, and Mr Poker-Man, who was as tall and as thin as a poker. Last of all went Roll-Around, who was as round as a ball, and rolled along instead of walking.

The two toys hid outside until all the

goodbyes were said, and then they crept out. They peered in at the window, and to their great surprise they saw the Little Wise Woman sitting on a chair, groaning and crying.

"Oh my!" she said. "I'm so tired, and there's all this mess to clear up before I go to bed."

The bear felt sorry for the unhappy little woman. He knocked on the door and went in.

"We will clear up everything for you," he said. "Don't worry. My friend Duck will make you a nice cup of tea, and a hot-water bottle, and I will sweep up the mess, clear the table, and wash up."

The Little Wise Woman was so surprised that she didn't know what to say.

"Where have you two come from?" she asked at last. "And why have you come to visit me tonight?"

"Never mind," said the bear, deciding not to talk about his own troubles now. "Why don't you snuggle into bed. Leave the rest to us."

"Grr-rrr!" growled the duck kindly, much to the Little Wise Woman's surprise.

"Quack!" said the bear, and surprised her still more. Then she remembered that her friend, the toyshop woman, had told her about a bear who quacked and a duck who growled, and she thought these must be the two strange toys. How kind they were to come and look after her like this, just when she had so much clearing up to do!

Before the Little Wise Woman went to get ready for bed, the duck made her a nice cup of tea, and gave her a hot-water bottle.

The bear was very busy, too. He cleared all the dirty dishes, washed them up, put them neatly away, and swept the floor. Then he put the cakes into their tins and the biscuits into their jars, and put the lids on.

He was very hungry, but of course he didn't dream of taking even half a biscuit. He knew it would be wrong, and he was a very good little bear.

"She's almost asleep," said the duck, peeking round the bedroom door. "We'd better go."

"I'm not quite asleep," said the Little Wise Woman, in a drowsy voice. "Before you go, look in my kitchen drawer. You will find two boxes of pills there. Bear, take a yellow pill, Duck, take a blue one. You won't be sorry you came to help me tonight."

"Thank you," said the bear, astonished.

He knew that the Little Wise Woman had many marvellous spells, and he wondered what would happen when he and the duck swallowed the pills.

Perhaps he would grow beautiful

whiskers, and maybe the duck would grow a wonderful tail.

He took a yellow pill, and the duck swallowed a blue one. Then they carefully shut the kitchen drawer, called goodnight to the Little Wise Woman and went out into the night.

They were very tired when they got back to the toyshop. They climbed up to their shelf, leaned back against the wall, and fell fast asleep at once.

They didn't wake up until the sun was shining into the shop. The doorbell woke them with a jump and they sat up. They saw the same little girl who had come to the shop the day before. She looked up at their shelf and pointed to them.

"I've come back to see that bear and duck again," she said.

The shopkeeper lifted them down. "It is a pity the duck growls and the bear quacks," she said.

She pressed the duck in the middle – and to everyone's enormous surprise the duck said "Quack!" very loudly indeed. The most surprised of all was the duck

herself. She had never in her life said "Quack", and it felt very funny indeed.

Then the little girl squeezed the bear, and to his delight he growled!

"Grr-rrr!" he went. Just like that.

"What a funny thing," said the little girl. "Have you had them mended?"

"No," said the shopkeeper, just as surprised as the little girl. "They've not been taken down from their shelf since you went out of the shop. I can't think what has happened to them."

The little girl pressed the bear and the duck again. "Grr-rrr!" growled the bear. "Quack!" said the duck. They were both most delighted. So that was what the pills from the Little Wise Woman had done – given them the right voices!

"Well, I will buy them now," said the little girl. "There's nothing wrong with them at all, and they are just what I wanted. I think the bear is lovely and the duck is a dear. I shall love them very much."

How pleased the two toys were when they heard that! When the shopkeeper popped them into a box they hugged one another hard – so hard that the duck had to say "Quack!" and the bear had to say "Grr-rrr!"

"Listen to that!" said the little girl, laughing. "They're saying that they're glad to come home with me."

Hurrah for
the Pepper-Pot!

Two families of mice lived in the old kitchen. One was Mrs Whisker Mouse's family and the other was Mrs Furry Mouse's.

They sometimes used to visit one another when the kitchen cat was not about. When Mrs Whisker's youngest mouse, Paddy-Paws, had a party, all Mrs Furry's children were most excited.

You should have seen the way that Mrs Furry dressed them up! The boys had red trousers and blue coats, the girls had tiny blue skirts and little shawls. They really looked most amusing.

They set off to the party. Mrs Furry first of all put her nose out of her hole to make quite sure the cat wasn't in the kitchen. She sniffed. She could smell no cat. But she could smell cheese up on the table! A meal was laid there for the farmer. Mrs Furry made up her mind that she would have a look at that cheese when the party was over. She set off across the kitchen with her little family.

The party was great fun. There were cheese cakes, bacon-rind sandwiches, and potato-peel pies. After the meal they all played games, and they squeaked and squealed so loudly that they didn't hear the big kitchen cat come stealing into the kitchen.

But he heard their squeaks and squeals! He blinked his big green eyes and sat himself down in a dark corner to wait until the mouse family came by.

When the party was over, Mrs Furry and her family came quietly out of Mrs Whisker's hole. "We'll just go up on to the table and see if we can nibble a bit of cheese!" whispered Mrs Furry to her four children. "Come along! We can climb up the tablecloth. It nearly touches the ground at the corners of the table."

So they all ran to the tablecloth and were up it in an instant! The cat was cross. It had hoped they were going straight to their hole. Then it could have caught them.

Now as the mice were climbing up to the table, Mrs Furry caught a smell of cat. She was frightened at once. Oh dear – where could the cat be? She stood on the table and sniffed and sniffed.

"The cat is somewhere about!" she whispered to her four children. "Keep up here with me. Don't move! Oh, if only I knew whether the cat is over there – or

by the sink – or sitting just by our own
hole! It is so dark that I can't see a
thing." The five mice sat as still as could
be. So did the cat. They were all listening
for each other. But nobody made a sound.
Not one single sound.

So the cat didn't know where the mice
were and the mice didn't know where
the cat was.

"Mother, surely we haven't got to stay
here all night!" whispered one of the
little mice. "Why when daylight comes,
we shall be easily seen."

"Oh dear, if only I knew where that
cat is!" said Mrs Furry. "How could I
find out?"

111

She ran a few steps over the tablecloth and bumped into something hard. It was the pepper-pot. And then Mrs Furry had a really splendid idea! She went back to her little family.

"Get out your hankies and bury your noses in them," she whispered. "I'm going to shake the pepper-pot as hard as I can, all around the edge of the table. Then if the cat is anywhere near, he will sneeze loudly when the pepper gets up his nose. But you mustn't sneeze and give away where we are – so get out your hankies!"

Then all the little mice got out their hankies and put their sharp little noses into them. Mrs Furry picked up the pepper-pot and ran to the edge of the table with it.

Shake-shake-shake! She emptied a whole lot of pepper on to the floor. Then she went to the other side. Shake-shake-shake! Down went some more yellow pepper, flying through the air. Shake-shake-shake! Shake-shake-shake!

And then a most tremendous sneeze

came up from the floor! The cat had got
some pepper up his nose and he simply
could not stop himself from sneezing!

"A-TISHOO!" he went, "A-TISHOO!"

Mrs Furry scampered back to her family. "The cat is over by the sink!" she whispered. "Come along, slip down this side of the table, and run for your hole!"

Down they all went and scampered across the kitchen as fast as they could go. The cat heard them, but another enormous sneeze came and nearly took his head off.

"A-TISHOO!" he went, just as the last mouse squeezed down the hole.

"Hurrah for the pepper-pot!" cried Mrs Furry.

And "Hurrah, hurrah!" cried all the little mice.

The
China Rabbit

On the playroom mantelpiece sat a little
china rabbit. It was a dear little thing,
with perky ears, a little white bobtail,
and two shining black eyes. It was not a
toy, but an ornament.

The two children, Anna and Freddy,
liked it very much. Their mother would
not let them play with it in case they
broke it.

"Leave it on the mantelpiece where it
looks nice," she said. "It's such a dear
little rabbit."

So the china rabbit lived on the
mantelpiece and was very happy. It
watched all that went on out of its
shining black eyes. The china rabbit saw
the most exciting things. There was
always something to look at.

Best of all was watching the toys come alive at night and play games on the floor. How the china rabbit longed to join them! But it wasn't a toy, so it couldn't. It just sat and watched. Sometimes it laughed out loud, because the teddy bear was very funny. He put on the dolls' bonnets, and rode on the clockwork mouse, and sometimes he fell off on purpose and rolled over and over on the floor, knocking down all the watching skittles as he went.

"Do it again!" the little china rabbit would cry. "Do it again!"

The toys were fond of the rabbit. The sailor doll often climbed up to talk to him. Rabbit listened carefully. But he never left the mantelpiece.

Now, one day a little imp came into the playroom from the mousehole, and all the toys stared at him in alarm. He really was very ugly and very unkind.

He was quick and nimble, and he skipped about, pulling the dolls' noses, tweaking the toy cat's fine whiskers, and tugging at the lamb's tail.

Then he saw the pretty talking-doll
hiding away in a corner, for she was very
frightened of the imp. The imp stared
at her in surprise. He had never seen
anyone quite so pretty and dainty. He
ran over to her and took her hand.

"Come with me to my mousehole," he
cried. "You can look after me!"

But the talking-doll said, "No, no, no!"
and ran to the sailor doll for help. Just
then the cock crowed – it was dawn.

The imp had to go, but before he went
he shouted, "I'll be back tomorrow. I'll
come and fetch you, Talking-Doll."

The toys were most upset. The next night they hid the talking-doll behind the big clock on the mantelpiece. It was a very good place. The china rabbit was pleased. He had always liked the little talking-doll. It was nice to have her nearby.

The sailor doll came up to the mantelpiece too, to take care of her. He sat beside the china rabbit and stroked his ears, telling him all kinds of news. Suddenly the imp popped out of the mousehole again.

"Here I am!" he cried gleefully. "Where's that pretty little doll? She is to come with me!"

Nobody answered. The imp was soon in a rage, for he guessed that she had been hidden. He ran to the brick-box and looked there, flinging out all the bricks. He ran to Mother's workbasket and looked there, throwing out the needles and cottons. He ran to the box of puzzles and looked there – you should have seen the playroom floor, quite covered with bits of puzzles by the time that imp had finished!

Now, he would never have found the talking-doll if she hadn't peeped out from behind the clock to see what was going on. As she popped her head out, the imp looked up and saw her.

"There she is!" he cried. "I've found her!"

He ran to the chair by the fireplace and began to climb up it. The sailor doll stood up and clenched his fists.

"Throw something at the imp!" cried the teddy bear from below. The sailor looked about for something to throw. There were three pennies on the mantelpiece. He picked one up. *Whizz!* It flew through the air, but the imp ducked and it missed him. The sailor threw another. That missed the imp too, and so did the third penny. The imp climbed steadily up. He would be on the mantelpiece in a moment.

There was a marble on the mantelpiece, too, left there by Freddy. Sailor Doll picked that up. *Whizz!* It flew through the air and hit the imp on the foot. He gave a yell of rage and shook his fist at the sailor.

"Go on, throw something else!" yelled the toys. "He's nearly there."

"There's nothing else to throw," shouted back poor Sailor Doll. "The clock's too heavy, and so is the moneybox."

"Throw me!" cried the china rabbit, suddenly. "Quick, Sailor, pick me up and throw me! I'll knock him down all right. I'll save the talking-doll."

"But you'll break," said the sailor.

"Never mind, just throw me! Oh, quickly, before it's too late!" shouted the rabbit.

So the sailor picked up the little china rabbit and hurled him at the imp, who was just about to climb on to the mantelpiece.

The rabbit flew straight for the imp. *Crash!* The imp landed in a crumpled heap on the floor! The rabbit fell to the ground too, but – oh dear! – he smashed into a hundred tiny bits. You couldn't tell which bit of him was ear or tail or nose or back – he was all in teeny-weeny scraps on the floor.

The toys were full of alarm. Poor little rabbit! Whatever could they do for him? They picked up all his bits and put them into a dish from the doll's-house. Then they looked at the imp. He lay on the floor looking dazed, with a great big bump on his head.

The bear fetched some string and tied his hands and feet. The imp struggled and tried to get up.

"Oh, no, you don't!" said the sailor doll. "You've been caught, Imp. We won't set you free until you promise to behave nicely."

"What hit me?" asked the imp, looking around.

"It was the poor china rabbit," said the teddy bear, sadly. "He was broken to pieces."

"Serves him right," said the imp.

"What a mean thing to say," said the sailor doll. "How would you like to be dropped out of the window and broken to pieces?"

"Oh no!" cried the imp, in fright. "You wouldn't do that, would you? Perhaps I can mend the rabbit for you. I have some magic glue here."

He sat up and the teddy untied his hands.

"If you can mend the rabbit, and you will promise to leave us alone from now on, we will set you free," said the sailor doll. "Here are the bits. Please put them together and get him right again."

The imp stared at the hundreds of tiny

bits in dismay. Then he set to work. He
worked all that night – and the next –
and soon the toys saw the shape of the
china rabbit coming again. The imp stuck
each tiny bit together in its right place.

During the daytime the toys kept him
inside the box of the jack-in-the-box, and
only let him out at night.

At last the china rabbit was back
together again. All the glue in the tube

was used. The toys gathered round the rabbit in delight.

"Welcome back, brave little china rabbit," they said. "Can you talk to us?"

The china rabbit found his tongue. It felt rather gluey, but he managed to talk.

"How's the talking-doll?" he asked.

"Quite well, thank you!" she said, and gave him a big hug. "Oh, Rabbit, it's nice to have you back again! It was dreadful when you were all in bits. You shall go back on the mantelpiece again tonight."

So up he went, carried carefully by the sailor doll, and there he stood once more, beaming down at everyone. As for the imp, he slipped away down the mouse-hole when no one was looking, but as everyone knew he would be much too frightened to come back again they took no notice.

Freddy and Anna were so pleased to see the china rabbit again. They had been very puzzled when he disappeared. They looked at him carefully and saw that he was covered with tiny, tiny cracks.

"Look, Mum," said Freddy, "he looks almost as if he had been broken into bits and mended again."

"Don't be silly," said his mother. "Who would mend him if he broke into tiny bits?"

The china rabbit stared at the children and longed to tell them who had mended him. But he didn't say a word.

He still sits there, just beside the clock. You'll see him if ever you go to play with Freddy and Anna. Don't forget to look for the tiny, tiny cracks all over him, will you?

The
Silver Merman

John was down by the seashore with his cousin Ella. He had been busy building sandcastles, when suddenly he noticed that Ella was crying.

"What's the matter, Ella?" he asked, throwing down his spade, and running over to her.

"I have lost my lovely ring," she sobbed.

"Where did you lose it?" asked John. "Let's go and hunt for it. I'm sure it won't take long to find."

"It's no use," said Ella, drying her eyes. "I lost it when I was out in the boat this morning. It fell off my finger as I was trailing my hand in the water, and before I could do anything, I saw it sinking down to the bottom of the sea."

"If only I knew the way there, I'd go and hunt for your ring," said John. "But I would drown if I went deep into the water."

"Of course you would, silly," said Ella, smiling. "Carry on building castles, and forget about my ring!"

John went off and thought hard as he dug in the sand.

"I'm sure I'd find that ring, if I could find someone to guide me under the sea," he said to himself.

"Well, I'll take you if you like!" said a sweet voice near him. John looked up in surprise. He saw a fairy sitting on a rock, with long hair blowing in the wind.

"I've never seen a fairy before!" he cried in delight. "Are you really a fairy?"

"Yes, really," she answered. "I'm on my way to visit my sister Pinkity, who married a merman. I heard what you said, as I was flying by, and I wondered if you'd like to come with me."

"Oh I would!" cried John. "Do please take me."

"Come along then," said the fairy,

holding out her hand. "My name's Sylfai. What's yours?"

"John," said the little boy. "That's my cousin Ella over there. She lost her ring in the waves, and I want to go down to the bottom of the sea so that I can look for it."

Sylfai led him into the water and it splashed over his socks. "Oh dear, I'll get wet!" he said. "I won't drown, will I?"

"Oh, I forgot," said Sylfai. "I must rub you with a sea-spell, so that you can walk beneath the water safe and dry. What a good thing you reminded me!"

She put her hands in the water and then made an outline round John's body, singing some strange magic words as she did so.

"There! Now you'll be all right!' she said. "Come along."

They ran into the water, deeper and deeper, until John was right up to his waist. It wasn't at all difficult to walk in the sea, like it usually is. Soon he was up to his shoulders, and then suddenly his head went right under! But he didn't splutter or choke. It was just as easy breathing in the water as on the land. John thought it was really wonderful. Bright fish swam all around them, and beautiful seaweed floated everywhere.

"We've a long way to go, so we'll find a fish to ride on," said Sylfai. She beckoned to a big codfish, and soon she and John were sitting comfortably on its back, racing through the water. *Swish! Swish!*

"I'm a little tired now," said the codfish at last. "Look, there's a crowd of jellyfish! Catch hold of the ribbons that hang down

from them, and they'll carry you as far as you want to go!"

"Please take us to Pinkity, the Silver Merman's wife!" cried Sylfai. The jelly-fish moved off quickly, and soon they arrived at a lovely cave, where a fairy sat combing out her long hair.

Sylfai let go of the jellyfish, and ran to kiss her little sister. John followed her, feeling rather shy.

"Oh, Sylfai, how lovely to see you!" cried Pinkity. "And who is this with you?"

"This is John," said Sylfai. "He's come to look for a lovely ring that his cousin has lost in the sea."

"But the sea is such a big place – it would take him all his life to find it!" cried Pinkity. "Never mind, John, maybe you could take her a pretty piece of coral instead."

"Where's your husband?" asked Sylfai.

"Oh, he's gone to the Ocean Market," said Pinkity. "He'll be back soon, in time for tea."

She set a cloth on a rock, and put a jug of pretty seaweed in the middle. Then

she put shells for plates, and cups made
of pink coral. John couldn't think how
anyone could drink out of a cup when
there was water all around, but Sylfai
said it was quite easy when you knew
how! John was looking forward to trying.

Soon the meal was ready, and they
took their places at the table. There was
seaweed soup, pink and green jelly made
from sea anemones, and starfish cakes.
John was very hungry and, though he
had never had such a strange meal
before, he enjoyed it very much.

"Here's my husband!" cried Pinkity.

John looked up, and saw a fine big merman swimming through the water. He had a tail like a fish, and gleamed like silver as he swam into the cave.

"Why, here's quite a party!" he said, chuckling. "Who's our guest?"

"I'm John," said John. "I'm very pleased to meet you."

"Same to you," said the merman, and he sat down at the table, and helped himself to some jelly. He was very friendly, and he told John such funny stories about the fish and crabs that the little boy could hardly eat for laughing.

"I bought you a present at the market,

Pinkity," said the merman. "It's something very special indeed! I paid a great many shells for it."

"Oh, show me!" cried Pinkity. The merman opened his hand and showed them a beautiful ring. John cried out in astonishment!

"Why, it's the very ring that my cousin Ella lost! It really is!"

"Dear me, is that so?" asked the merman. "It came down from the surface of the water this morning, and was taken to the market to be sold by the fish who found it."

"Yes, and Ella lost hers this morning!" cried John. "So it must be the same one. What a very peculiar thing!"

"Well, you must take it back to Ella," said Pinkity. "I couldn't keep it now I know that."

"Oh, no," said John, "your husband bought it, and he must give it to you. I'll tell Ella, and I'm sure she'll be pleased when she knows you have got it."

"No, you must take it," said the merman.

But John wouldn't, no matter how they begged him to. He was quite sure Ella would rather Pinkity had it.

"I really ought to go back now," he said. "Ella will be worried."

"I'll take you to the shore on one of my white horses!" said the merman. "They go very fast indeed."

He swam off, and soon came back with a beautiful horse, whose white mane streamed like foam in the water.

"I never knew that the white waves I saw rolling in to shore were really and truly the manes of horses!" said John in surprise.

The merman helped him up, and then sat on the horse behind him sideways, for his tail was rather awkward to manage on horseback.

"Goodbye!" called John, waving to Sylfai and Pinkity.

The white horse rose to the surface of the water and then, with its foamy mane just showing above the waves, began to gallop along swiftly.

Poor Ella had suddenly missed John,

and was dreadfully worried about him. She was walking up and down by the sea, calling him. A host of little fish put their heads above the water and told her not to worry, but of course she couldn't understand a word they said. She wasn't under a sea-spell, like John.

The white horse rushed out on the beach, and John jumped off. Before he

could call goodbye and thank the merman, the horse had turned, and vanished once more. John went to look for Ella.

There she was, way along the beach, calling at the top of her voice: "John, John, where are you?"

"Here I am!" called John, and he raced up to her.

"Oh, John, where have you been?" asked Ella. "I have been so worried about you."

"I've been to the bottom of the sea to look for your ring," said John. "And do you know, the Silver Merman had bought it for Pinkity! They wanted me to take it to you, but I said I knew you would much rather Pinkity had it, and I made them keep it."

"What are you talking about?" said Ella. "Don't tell stories, John! Nobody can go to the bottom of the sea, except divers."

"But I did go!" said John sticking his hands into his pockets, as he always did when he was cross.

"Well, I don't believe you," said Ella. "You've just been hiding somewhere to give me a fright."

"I haven't," said John – and then a strange look came over his face. He had felt something peculiar at the bottom of one of his pockets. He pulled it out – and there was the ring!

"Goodness!" he said, in astonishment. "The merman must have slipped it into my pocket when I was in front of him

on the white horse! Look Ella! Here's your ring – now I expect you'll believe me, won't you!"

Ella took the ring with a cry of delight, and slipped it on her finger. "I shall have to believe you!" she said. "You really are a dear to find it for me!"

Then off they went together, and John spent the rest of the day telling Ella all about his exciting adventures with his new friends under the sea.

Mr Quink's Garden

One fine day, not long ago, Mr Brown took his wife and children, Jenny and Tom, for a day out in the country.

"It will be a lovely day," said Mr Brown. "The countryside is beautiful at this time of year. We'll have lots of fun together. Let's hurry up and pack a big picnic."

So they made ham and tomato sandwiches, and packed them into lunch boxes. They took two bottles of home-made lemonade, and packed oranges and bananas into a basket with the bottles. They took a large fruitcake and a packet of biscuits. And last of all they took four bars of chocolate and a bag of sweets.

It was a lovely day when they set off in the car. The sun shone and the sky was

141

as blue as the bluebells in the woods. Birds sang in the hedges, and the banks were yellow with primroses.

The Brown family were happy, sitting and looking at the scenery.

They got out of the car at last and walked into the woods. The sun was so hot that they were glad of the shade. Tom and Jenny ran on in front, shouting to their mother to look at the bluebells. Mr and Mrs Brown carried the bags and basket.

"Look for a nice place to sit, Jenny," called Mrs Brown.

Presently they found just the spot. It was the prettiest place in the wood – and, although they did not know it, it was the garden belonging to Mr Quink, the brownie. He lived in the old oak-tree under whose branches the Brown family sat. He had a close-fitting door in the trunk of the tree and a small window with a tiny curtain of moss. No one knew he lived there – except the little folk of course – for Mr Quink never showed himself to ordinary people.

Now Mr Quink was very proud of his garden and he worked there every night. There was a tiny stream running through it, and he had planted flowers neatly along each bank. He had arranged cushions of moss so that his friends could sit on them when they came to visit him. He had three patches of bluebells, the finest in the wood – and a white bluebell, which is a very lucky flower. Mr Quink planted honeysuckle in one corner, and a nook of violets close by, so that whoever sat there could smell the sweet scent of the hidden violets. Everything in the garden was neat, tidy and beautiful.

No wonder the Browns thought it was lovely! They sat down under the tree and put their baskets by the trunk. They didn't know they were in a brownie's garden, as there was no fence or hedge round it.

"Let's have our lunch now," said Mrs Brown, beginning to unpack the things. Soon they were all munching happily. They drank the lemonade. It was delicious.

"Let's put the bottles over there and throw stones at them," said Mr Brown.

"But won't the broken pieces be dangerous?" said Mrs Brown.

"Who for? No one ever comes here," said Mr Brown.

So they set up the bottles and threw stones at them, and soon the bottles were smashed to bits, and pieces of glass lay all over the ground. Mr Brown unfolded his newspaper. "I'm going to have a rest," he said. "Run along and play, children."

Little by little the lovely garden belonging to Mr Quink began to look dreadful. The brownie peeped out of his tiny window in the oak tree and saw with dismay what was happening.

He saw Mrs Brown peel oranges for the children and throw the peel on the ground. He saw the children eating bananas and throwing the skins at one another. And he saw Mr Brown throw empty sweet wrappers under the honey-suckle bush.

The Brown family stayed there all afternoon. It was so peaceful, and the

birds sang sweetly. They had tea and then it was time to go home.

Mrs Brown looked round at the mess, and couldn't help feeling a bit sorry about it.

"Are there any litter bins?" she asked. "Perhaps we ought to clear this mess up."

"There aren't any, Mum," said Tom. "This is quite a wild part of the wood. I don't suppose anyone comes here but us. Still, our teacher always tells us not to spoil the country – don't you think we should take our rubbish back home with us?"

"I'm not carrying all that litter back," said Mr Brown. He was rather a selfish man. "Leave it here. No one will ever know."

"Mummy, let's take these bluebells home with us," cried Jenny. "And let's dig up the primroses and violets, and some of the moss. We can plant them in our garden at home!"

So they dug up Mr Quink's finest primroses, violets and moss, and picked

all his bluebells – and then they found the lucky white bluebell! So they dug it up and put it in the basket too. Then home they went.

Mr Quink opened his front door and crept out. When he saw his beautiful garden scattered with broken glass, orange-peel, banana skins, cardboard boxes, empty bags and packets, sweet papers and sheets of newspaper – when he saw his lovely plants gone and his moss spoilt, he sat down on a stone and cried big tears. But when he found his white bluebell gone he was very angry!

He called a meeting of all the brownies in the wood and they came to see his spoilt garden. Most of them had complaints and grumbles too.

"Some people left all their horrible paper bags in my field the other day," said Nod, an old brownie.

"And some boys threw broken bottles into my stream, and I cut my feet when I paddled there," said Doolin, a small, bright-eyed brownie.

"But these Browns are the worst of the lot," said Mr Quink fiercely. "Look at this mess! Whatever shall I do with it?"

"Well, the Browns have a neat little garden," said Hoodle, a sharp-eyed brownie who travelled a good deal. "As all this mess belongs to them, why not take it back to them and put it into their own garden?"

"That's a good idea!" said all the brownies at once. "They don't seem to mind litter and rubbish and mess – so maybe they won't bother about broken bottles and papers and peel in their own garden."

"I can give them some newspapers I've picked up in my field," said Nod.

"And I can give them a sackful of broken glass," said Doolin.

"We'll go tonight and dump everything in the Browns' garden," said everyone. "How pleased they will be to get such a nice lot of rubbish back!"

That night they took their sacks and made their way from the wood, riding on the back of the midnight owl who flies to and from the town.

When they got to the Browns' garden they landed on the grass and opened their sacks. They shook glass all over the neat lawn. They threw newspapers where the wind could blow them around. They scattered paper and boxes and peel and skin here and there. Just as they were going, Mr Quink stopped and pointed to something.

"Look!" he said. "My lucky white bluebell! I'll take that back with me."

"And see – here's a lupin plant just flowering!" said Nod. "I haven't got one of those at home. As the Browns took your flowers, Quink, they probably wouldn't mind us taking theirs. I'd like that lupin!"

In a few minutes the brownies were digging up all the nicest things in the Browns' garden, and then off they went again on the owl, their sacks empty of rubbish but full of lovely plants. They were delighted.

In the morning, when Mr Brown woke up and looked out of the window, he got such a shock! His garden was a wreck! The plants were gone, the lawn was scattered with broken glass, and all kinds of rubbish blew about or lay on the flower beds.

"Just look at that!" said Mr Brown fiercely. "Now who's done that, I should like to know?"

Mrs Brown jumped out of bed and gazed at the dreadful garden. Tears came into her eyes, for she loved her little garden. "Oh, how could anyone be so horrid?" she said.

Tom and Jenny were angry too. "What a terrible mess," said Jenny. "Why don't people clear up their litter properly instead of throwing it into our garden?"

Mr Brown told the policeman, who wrote a lot of things down in his note-book and said he would keep a watch on the garden and see it didn't happen again. And Tom and Jenny spent the whole morning clearing up the mess and making the garden neat. Mr Brown had to buy more plants in place of the ones that had gone, and he was very angry about it.

The next night, although the police-man watched carefully, someone he didn't see came and emptied all sorts of rubbish in the Browns' garden again! It was most extraordinary because although the policeman saw the rubbish being thrown about the garden he couldn't see who was throwing it!

The brownies were invisible to him,

for he didn't believe in fairies. He was frightened and ran all the way back to the police station.

And do you know, the brownies still come every other night or so and give to the Browns all the rubbish that people leave in the countryside. Their garden is a dreadful sight and they can't do anything about it.

In fact, Jenny is beginning to wonder if it can be the little folk who are doing it – and she wishes her family hadn't been so untidy in the wood that day!

"I shall put up a notice to say we're sorry and won't spoil the country again," said Jenny. "Then the little folk will stop bringing us rubbish." So she is going to do that tonight – and then the brownies will have to choose someone else's garden. I hope it won't be yours!

But I'm sure you are not like the Browns, are you? You know how to behave when you go to the country, so *your* garden will be safe!

Jumbo
Saves the Day

Outside the playroom window, inside an old flowerpot, lived three small pixies called Briar, Berry and Buttercup. The toys knew them very well indeed, for the pixies often came into the playroom at night when it was dark, and played with them.

Briar and Berry were big strong pixies, but Buttercup was small and sweet. She was their sister, and they loved her very much. All the toys loved her too, and they let her ride in the wooden train, and the toy motor-car, and even on the big rocking-horse as many times as she liked.

Buttercup liked all the toys except big Jumbo, the grey elephant. He had once trodden on her toe by accident, and now she was frightened of him. Jumbo was sad about this, because he liked Buttercup very much, and was always longing to give her a ride on his back. But she never would ride on him, for he was too big and clumsy.

The toys belonged to two children called Amy and Andrew, but lately the children hadn't bothered to play with their toys very often. Their Uncle Jim had given them something they liked much better – two pairs of roller-skates! You should have seen how the two children tore round and round on them! Goodness, they went like lightning!

The toys were jealous of the roller-skates. The children kept them in the toy-cupboard but every night the toys pushed them out.

"They are nasty things," said the clockwork clown, giving the skates a push. "I don't know why the children like them better than they like us. Get out of the toy-cupboard, you ugly things! You don't belong in here!"

Then *bump-bump*! Out would tumble

the four skates on to the floor. They weren't alive, so they didn't mind one way or another. But the children were always puzzled to know how it was their skates fell out of the toy-cupboard so often!

So every night the toys were very glad when the three pixies came to join them.

"It's nice to have somebody to play with," said the teddy bear. "The children hardly ever take any notice of us now!"

Then one night Berry and Briar came in through the window in a great hurry, looking as scared as could be.

"Toys, toys! Whatever shall we do? Six

naughty red goblins came tonight and stole away Buttercup, our little pixie sister! Oh, whatever shall we do?"

The toys turned pale with fright. Even the teddy bear, who was the bravest of all of them, looked quite white, so you can guess how frightened they all were. No one liked the red goblins.

They were very naughty and liked nothing better than to play nasty tricks on people. They had once poured glue all over the playroom windowsill in the hope that one of the toys would get stuck there. Another time they had stolen pieces from all the children's jigsaws so that none could be finished completely. And now they had taken away Buttercup! Whatever could be done?

"They'll have taken her back to Goblin Land!" said the panda. "That's a long way from here!"

"Well, you can't ask me to go after them," said the clockwork train, in a hurry. "I can only run on my rails."

"And my key is lost," said the clockwork motor-car. "I can't go!"

"Nobody wants to go!" wailed the two pixies sorrowfully. "Poor Buttercup! She'll never come back again."

Then Jumbo spoke up in his big, deep voice. "I will go and chase those goblins!" he said. "I'm not afraid!"

"Dear old Jumbo!" cried all the toys together. "What a kind, brave elephant you are! But you're so slow and clumsy it would take you ages to get there."

"Ah, but I've got a splendid idea!" said Jumbo. "I want you to strap those roller-skates on to my big feet. Then, if you'll help me to practise, I shall go like the wind, roller-skating down the paths to Goblin Land!"

Well, what an idea! Did you ever hear

anything like it! An elephant on roller-skates! Anyway, you should have seen how the toys and the two pixies clapped their hands when they heard what Jumbo said. They thought it was the best idea they had ever heard.

"Quick! Get the roller-skates!" cried Berry.

"Where are they?" cried Briar.

Panda got one, Teddy found another, and the two biggest dolls brought the last two. Then they strapped them on to Jumbo's big, clumsy feet. He did look funny!

"I'm just going to have a skate round the playroom to see if I can do it properly," said Jumbo, shaking with excitement. And off he went, round and round the room.

Crash! Crash! Crash! went his feet, as he tried his hardest to skate with all four at once. Dear me, you should have seen him!

All the toys got out of his way in a great hurry, for his four feet shot out all over the place, and he didn't know where

he was going. He knocked the clockwork
clown flat on his nose and ran over the
teddy bear's big toe. Goodness, it was a
sight to see!

"Steady on, Jumbo!" called Berry,
jumping up on to a chair for safety. But as
soon as he sat down, Jumbo bounced
into the chair and sent it flying! Down fell

poor Berry with a crash. Up he got and climbed up on to the windowsill, feeling certain that Jumbo couldn't knock that down!

After a little while Jumbo began to skate much better. His legs went properly and he found that he could skate right round the playroom and back again without falling over once. He did feel proud.

"Now, I'm ready to go after Buttercup and the goblins," he said to the pixies. "Jump up on my back and tell me the right way to go."

So Berry and Briar jumped up on to his broad back, and hung on tightly. *Crash! Crash! Crash!* went the roller skates as

Jumbo skated out of the room and down the passage that led to the garden. What a noise he made! It's a wonder he didn't wake the whole house up!

Berry and Briar soon managed to unlock the back door and the three of them slipped out into the garden. The moon was shining brightly as Jumbo went skating splendidly down the garden path.

If one of his feet slipped he still had three others to help him so he didn't fall over at all.

He did go at a rate! Out into the lane he skated and over the hill, until he came to the extra-large rabbit-hole that was the entrance to Goblin Land.

The streets of Goblin Land are very straight and smooth, so soon Jumbo found he could go even faster! *Crash! Crash! Crash!* went his skates and he tore along faster than any motor-car could possibly go. Berry and Briar soon lost their hats, for the wind streamed past them and snatched away their hats with greedy fingers.

"There they are, there they are!" shouted Berry suddenly, so loudly that he frightened Briar and nearly made him fall off Jumbo's back. Jumbo looked in front of him and saw, far in the distance, a crowd of little red goblins riding yellow rocking-horses. One of them held Buttercup tightly in his arms, while he shouted to his rocking-horse to rock faster and faster through Goblin Land.

Jumbo made a sound like a trumpet and skated on faster than ever. The goblins heard the crash of his skates and looked back. When they saw Jumbo roller-skating behind them, carrying Berry and Briar on his back, they could hardly believe their eyes. They shouted loudly to their rocking-horses.

"Go on! Go on! You must go faster still! Hurry, hurry, hurry!"

The rocking-horses rocked away till it seemed as if they must tumble on their noses or tails. They went very fast indeed. But Jumbo went even faster. How he skated! You could hardly see his legs moving, they went so quickly.

"They're taking Buttercup to the Deep Green Cave!" cried Berry suddenly. "Oh dear, catch them before they get there, Jumbo, or we shall never see our dear little sister again!"

Sure enough, they were heading straight for the Deep Green Cave, the place where all the goblins' nastiest magic is made. Jumbo skated even faster to get there before the goblins did – and he got there with just a single second to spare.

Now, luckily, Jumbo was so big that he easily blocked the entrance to the Deep Green Cave. And as the first goblin came rocking towards him, Jumbo scooped him up in his big, long trunk and left him dangling in the branches of a nearby tree.

He did the same with the second, and the third goblin, and the other three were so frightened by the big, brave elephant that they soon started rocking in the opposite direction. But not before Jumbo had gently rescued Buttercup, of course!

"On my back, quick, all of you!"

shouted Jumbo, in his trumpeting voice, for he was sure that the red goblins would soon be back with some nasty magic to help them.

Berry jumped up. Then it was Buttercup's turn. She had quite forgotten that she had said she would never, ever ride on Jumbo's back, so she got up as quickly as ever she could, and Briar followed close behind her.

Then back went Jumbo through Goblin Land, skating as fast as his four legs would carry him. Long before the red goblins came running after them, Jumbo was out of sight, crash-crash-crashing along on his four roller-skates! It didn't take him long to get back to the playroom, very much out of breath, but simply delighted that Buttercup was safely home again. The toys gave him a great welcome, and cheered him with all their might. His trunk blushed quite red with pride.

The toys unstrapped the skates from his tired feet and put them away again. Then they heard the first cock crowing to say that day was coming, so they hurriedly said goodbye to the pixies and climbed back into the toy-cupboard to go to sleep.

Berry and Briar patted Jumbo before they went, but Buttercup flung her arms round his trunk and kissed him lovingly.

"You're a dear, brave Jumbo," she said, "and I'm sorry I ever said you were clumsy. I'll come and ride on you every single night if you'll let me!"

Then off she went, and left Jumbo standing by himself, very happy indeed. And he was happier still the night after, for Buttercup came back and kept her promise. Good old Jumbo carried her all around the playroom and she wasn't frightened at all, no, not even for a minute!

The
Wishing Hat

Spillikins the pixie went into Dame Twinkle's teashop for tea. He took off his pointed cap and hung it up on a hook behind his chair. Then he ordered tea.

He looked round the shop. There were quite a lot of people there. He saw See-Saw the wizard, eating sardines on gingerbread, a meal he liked very much. He saw Whistler the gnome drinking pink lemonade. And in the corner were Flip and Flap, the goblins, eating egg pie as fast as they could.

Spillikins was in rather a hurry so he asked for a glass of cold milk and a bun. He knew they wouldn't take very long to prepare. He munched his bun, and when it was finished he drank his milk down to the last drop. Then he paid his bill, took

170

his cap off the hook, popped it on his head, and off he went.

It was a bright and beautiful sunny day and Spillikins whistled cheerily as he thought of the day ahead. He was going to see his friend Tippy, who lived in a lovely little cottage all by himself. Spillikins was going to help him to weed his garden. Tippy lived a long way away, and Spillikins soon got hot walking along in the sunshine that streamed over the fields.

"I wish somebody would come to wheel me in a barrow all the way there," he

said to himself. "I'm getting jolly hot."

Just as he said that he heard something trundling behind him. He turned round – and what a funny thing! There was a big green wheelbarrow being pushed by an imp. He knocked Spillikins into the barrow and began to wheel him along.

"Ooh!" said Spillikins, in surprise. "He must have heard what I said, and decided to give me a ride. Well, this is better than walking."

The imp pushed him along, over the field and down the lanes. Spillikins liked it – but the barrow was very hard to sit in, especially when it bumped over stones.

"I do wish I had a nice cushion or something to sit on," he said. "I'm getting quite bruised."

No sooner had he said the words than to his enormous surprise a huge yellow cushion appeared under him in the barrow! It was so soft and comfortable. Spillikins stared at it in amazement.

"Well, where did you come from?" he

asked. "Hi, imp! Did you put this cushion here?"

But the imp said nothing. He just went on wheeling the barrow. Spillikins looked puzzled. There was something funny about the imp and the sudden way he had appeared.

"I am hot!" sighed the pixie, as the sun shone down hotter than ever. "I wish it would rain lemonade. How nice it would . . ."

He stopped suddenly. A great yellow cloud had blown over the sun, and large yellow drops of rain had started to fall all around.

"Buttons and buttercups!" cried Spillikins in astonishment, "I do believe it is raining lemonade. Ooh, what a funny thing!"

He opened his mouth and let the drops fall on to his tongue. They were delicious. Real, sweet lemonade, the nicest he had ever tasted. But after a while Spillikins began to feel wet, for the lemonade shower was a heavy one.

"I wish it would stop," he said. "I'm getting wet through."

In an instant the lemonade rain stopped and the sky became blue again. Spillikins looked very thoughtful. It was turning into a very strange day indeed.

"It seems to me as if all my wishes are coming true," he said. "I wonder why. Well, I'll wish a few more and see if they come true too."

He thought for a moment. Then he wished.

"I wish I had a carriage made of gold, drawn by three giraffes," he said.

Immediately a shining carriage stood before him, and in front were three tall

giraffes! Spillikins was delighted. He jumped out of the wheelbarrow and ran to the carriage.

"I wish for a lion to drive my carriage and two kangaroos for footmen," he said.

Immediately, the wish came true. A lion sat on the box, dressed in a wonderful coachman's uniform, and two kangaroos dressed as footmen stood up behind.

"Now I wish for a suit of gold and a cloak of silver," said Spillikins. "Ha! Here they are! Don't I look grand!"

He got into the carriage and told the lion to drive to his friend Tippy's house. He wished for all sorts of animals to follow him, all dressed in silver tunics and each carrying a present for his friend, and to his great delight they appeared, looking very grand indeed. There was an elephant, a camel with a present between his humps, a big furry panda and even an ostrich!

"That will make Tippy stare," thought Spillikins in delight. "He's always boasting about this, that and the other – but he won't boast any more when he sees me! I've only got to wish and I can have anything I want!"

He was so excited that he could hardly wait to get to Tippy's. When at last the giraffe coach drew up outside his friend's cottage, he saw Tippy in the garden. But as soon as Tippy saw the lion coachman, the giraffes, and the kangaroo footmen, he dropped his spade and fled indoors, frightened out of his life!

"Hi, Tippy! Tippy! Don't be afraid!" cried Spillikins. "It's only me! Guess

what! All my wishes are coming true!"

He ran indoors after Tippy and told him everything that had happened, and at last his friend believed him. He kept staring and staring at Spillikins in his gold tunic and silver cloak, and he wondered how it was that the pixie had managed to make his wishes come true.

"I don't know *how* it is," said Spillikins. "I really don't. It must just be some wonderful magic that has grown in me."

"Take off your hat and sit down," said Tippy. "You have had such a busy day. And besides, we don't need to do any weeding. We can just wish all the weeds away, and our work will be done. Ha ha!"

"Ha ha!" said Spillikins, and he pulled off his pointed cap.

"I say!" he said, staring at it. "This cap isn't mine! I must have taken the wrong one at the teashop. No wonder it felt so tight! It doesn't fit me at all well, and has given me quite a headache. I wish I had my own cap instead."

Whoooooooosh! Almost before he had finished speaking, the cap he was holding flew away suddenly and another cap fell into Spillikins' hands. It was his own! But oh dear me, at the very same moment away went his silver cloak and gold tunic, leaving him in his plain old

clothes. Off galloped the giraffe coach, and after it went all the animals with the presents Spillikins had brought for Tippy!

"Oh my, what's happening?" cried Spillikins, all of a tremble. "Hi! I wish you all to come back."

But alas! They didn't come back. They had gone for good!

"Oh dear, dear, dear!" sobbed Spillikins in the greatest disappointment. "I know what's happened. I must have taken Wizard See-Saw's hat by mistake, when I left the teashop. It was a wishing-cap – and that's why all the wishes I wished came true. Now I've got my own cap back I've lost the wishing power!"

"Oh!" groaned Tippy, getting up. And to think we might have wished all those weeds away! Why didn't we when we had the chance? Come along out, Spilly, and do some work."

Out they went, two very sad little pixies. That night they both dreamed of lions, kangaroos and giraffes – and I don't wonder at it, do you?

Twinkle's
Fur Coat

There was once an elf who wanted a fur coat. Her friend Ripple the pixie had one, and so had old Goody Tiptap over the road.

"I want one too!" sighed Twinkle the elf. "A fur coat looks so nice, and keeps people so warm, Ripple, was your fur coat very much money to buy?"

"Yes, very, very much," said Ripple. "It took a whole year's savings."

"Goody Tiptap, was your fur coat expensive to buy?" asked Twinkle, as Goody came by.

"It belonged to my mother," said Goody Tiptap. "Her brother was a hunter, and he brought home the skins for a coat. I do not know if it would be dear to buy."

Twinkle counted out the money in her money-box, but she didn't have much at all in it.

"Certainly not enough to buy a fur coat," thought Twinkle sadly.

She put the money back into her money-box. "I shan't think any more about a fur coat," she said. "I shall go and call on my Aunt Tabitha and take her some flowers out of my garden – that is, if I can find any! The poor things are dying because we haven't had any rain for so long."

She found some flowers and made them into a nice bunch. Then she set off to her aunt's. On the way there she

heard a good deal of squeaking, and she crept through the grass to see what it was all about.

She peeped from behind a buttercup – and in a circle of grass, she saw twelve furry caterpillars holding a meeting.

"Good gracious!" said Twinkle in surprise. "I never saw caterpillars holding a meeting before. I wonder what it's all about?"

So she went to see. The caterpillars turned to her as she spoke. "Whatever's the matter?" she asked

"We're worried!" said the largest furry caterpillar. "Do you know, all our food-plants are dying for want of rain, and we haven't enough to eat!"

"Really!" said Twinkle, surprised. "Well, what are you going to do?"

"We don't know," said the caterpillar sadly. "We could go and find some other place where the plants are better perhaps – but we don't know which way we had better go."

"What sort of plants do you want?" asked Twinkle.

"Well, we like plantains and nettles –
and lettuce is a big treat, although we
hardly ever get it," said the biggest
caterpillar waving his black head at
Twinkle.

"Now listen," said Twinkle. "I'm going
for a walk to my Aunt Tabitha's. On the
way I will see if I can find any good food-
plants for you to eat. Maybe I can find
some in a ditch, where it is damp. I will
tell you if I do, and show you the way
there."

"Oh, thank you," said the big
caterpillar. "You see, it is nearly time for

us to change into chrysalises and sleep, but we do need a good meal first."

Twinkle set off. All the way to her aunt's she kept a look-out for some nice, juicy, green plants for the hungry caterpillars – but alas, everything looked dry and dead. No rain had fallen for three weeks, and the plants were dying.

"Isn't it dreadful," thought Twinkle as she set off back home again. Her aunt was out, so Twinkle had just popped into the kitchen and put her flowers in water on the table. "Isn't it dreadful. No food for the poor caterpillars! All the plantains are dead and dry, and the nettles are grey instead of green! How everything does want rain."

She came back to the caterpillars. She looked at them sadly and shook her head.

"It's sad," she said. "But everywhere is the same. There isn't a thing for you to eat!"

"Then we shall die," said the biggest caterpillar. "And oh, what a pity it is, because after one more good feed we should each be ready to turn into a chrysalis, and sleep there until we had changed into a beautiful tiger moth."

"Oh, do you turn into those lovely red-and-black tiger moths?" cried Twinkle in excitement. "The Fairy Queen has those to ride on when she goes for a moonlight flight! I've seen her – and once she let me ride on one of her tiger moths,

and it was lovely! It fluttered its big coloured wings and off we went into the air!"

"Well, I'm afraid the Queen will not have many tiger moths to ride this year," said the big caterpillar. "If only we could get something green and juicy to eat – but it's no use if you say that everywhere is dried up."

"Listen!" said Twinkle suddenly. "I will tell you what to do. I have a lettuce-bed, and you shall come with me and eat some of my lettuces. Then you will each be able to turn into a chrysalis and the Queen will have her tiger moths to ride on."

"Oh, thank you, Twinkle!" squeaked all the caterpillars. Then, with Twinkle leading the way, they all followed her in a long furry line, their dark brown bodies going up and down as they walked over the field.

What a feast those caterpillars had in Twinkle's lettuces! Twinkle really was surprised to see how much they could eat. Their jaws opened and shut as they

chewed the green lettuce leaves, and soon there were very, very few lettuces left. Twinkle was rather sad. She hadn't thought that caterpillars could eat so much!

The next day the big caterpillar spoke to her. "Thank you," he said. "Thank you! Now we shall not eat any more. Our time has come for each of us to turn into a chrysalis."

"May I watch you?" asked Twinkle. "It always seems such a strange and powerful magic to me when a caterpillar changes into a chrysalis and then comes out of the chrysalis as a moth or butterfly! How does your caterpillar body change into a moth's body with lovely big wings, Caterpillar?"

"We don't know," said the furry caterpillar. "It is a strange spell, but we don't understand it. Of course you can watch us, little elf. You have been very kind to us. Now, are you ready, caterpillars? Then first of all take off your furry skins. You will not want those in the chrysalis!"

So every caterpillar shed its furry coat – and there were all the little furs lying on the ground! The elf suddenly gave a cry of delight, and shouted to the caterpillars:

"Don't you want your furry skins any more? Can I have them, please?"

"Of course," said the big caterpillar. "If you don't have them I expect the mice will come along and eat them, or the beetles. Whatever do you want them for?"

"Ah, you will see when you change into moths and come creeping out of your chrysalises!" said Twinkle.

She collected all the furry skins and ran off to the house with them. She washed them well. She hung them on the line to dry. She took her needle and thimble and thread and she began to sew.

How she sewed! She sewed all those little furry caterpillar skins together, and made a beautiful warm fur coat from them! You should have seen it! It fitted her beautifully, and was so warm and cosy.

When she had finished the coat, she

shook it out and then went to see what had happened to the caterpillars. They were all fast asleep in tight black chrysalis cases! Twinkle touched one – and it wriggled.

"They are alive but sleeping," said the elf. "How strange that they are growing into moths while they sleep! I will wait until they awake – and then I will show them my fur coat."

Weeks later the caterpillars awoke, each in his hard little chrysalis case – but they were no longer caterpillars! They had changed into magnificent moths – tiger moths with bright red, cream, and black wings, beautiful to see!

Twinkle watched each moth make a hole in its case and creep out. Their wings were damp and crumpled but in an hour or two each moth had dried its lovely wings and was fluttering them in the air.

"Oh, do you remember me?" cried the elf, dancing up to them. "You knew me when you were furry caterpillars. You gave me your furry skins when you took

them off for the last time! Look at the
lovely fur coat I made from your skins!"

The bright moths looked, and waved
their feelers about.

"Yes, we remember you," said the
biggest moth. "You were the elf who
helped us – and we are glad we gave you
our skins to make you a fur coat. You
deserve it! We will give you a ride too,
any night you want one. You are a kind
little thing."

They spread their wings and flew off to the Fairy Queen; but sometimes, when the Queen spares one, he flies off to Twinkle, and gives her a ride through the moonlit wood. She puts on her warm fur coat then, and looks perfectly sweet.

Wasn't it a cheap fur coat? It only cost a few lettuces and a bit of kindness!